Adrienne Thompson

Pink Cashmere Publishing

Arkansas, USA

Cover created by Adrienne Thompson

Cover Image: © Mona Makela | Dreamstime.com

All rights reserved.

This book or any portion thereof may not be reproduced or used in any manner whatsoever without the express written permission of the publisher except for the use of brief quotations in a book review.

This is a work of fiction. Names, characters, businesses, places, events, and incidents are either the products of the author's imagination or used in a fictitious manner. Any resemblance to actual persons, living or dead, or actual events is purely coincidental.

Printed in the United States of America

First Printing 2014

Copyright © 2014 Adrienne Thompson

ISBN: 0988871378

ISBN-13: 978-0-9888713-7-3

Acknowledgments

To the Most High, the One True God, my Lord and Savior: thank You for saving me over and over again. Thank You for loving and keeping me. Thank You for knowing me even when I didn't know You.

To my readers: I truly don't know what to say other than thank you. You have accepted my work over and over again. You've been willing passengers on my wild literary rides. You've bought my books, spread the word, left reviews, sent me messages, and without even realizing it, you've kept me from giving up. I pray that something I've written has blessed you in some way. THANK YOU.

A special thank you to Sharon Blount, the Building Relationships Around Books Online Book Club, and the Black Pearls Book Club of North Texas, as well as all of the other book clubs that have chosen to read my work. I am truly honored.

Thank you, Tonja Tate, for being a wonderful beta reader!

A special thank you to my mother, Bobbie Conaway. Thank you for always helping me even though I'm good and grown, lol. I love you.

"He heals the brokenhearted and binds up their wounds."

Psalm 147:3 NIV

Soundtrack:

"Epiphany" Chrisette Michele

"Like A Dream" Chrisette Michele

"Goodbye Game" Chrisette Michele

"Mine" Ledisi

"Get Through the Night" Chrisette Michele

"Fragile" Chrisette Michele

"Be Ok" Chrisette Michele featuring will.i.am

"Another One" Chrisette Michele

"On My Own" Chrisette Michele

"Excuse Me" Jazmine Sullivan

"Trippin'" Ledisi

"Pray Me Well" Chrisette Michele featuring Rob Glasper

"Coffee" Ledisi

"Pieces of Me" Ledisi

"What You Do" Chrisette Michele

"Goin' Thru Changes" Ledisi

"Unsaid" Chrisette Michele

"Lost and Found (Find Me)" Ledisi

"Better" Chrisette Michele

Soundtrack Continued:

"Golden" Chrisette Michele

"The Way" Jill Scott

"Blame It on Me" Chrisette Michele

"Knockin'" Ledisi

"Turn Me Loose" Ledisi

"Late Nights & Early Mornings" Marsha Ambrosius

"I Don't Know Why, But I Do" Chrisette Michele

"My Heart" Chrisette Michele featuring Lem Payne

"Upside Down" Ledisi

"All I Ever Think About" Chrisette Michele

"A Couple of Forevers" Chrisette Michele

1

"Epiphany"

When you've been through what I've been through—what I like to call the "ultimate betrayal"—you start to think a little too much. You start to rehash things your significant other said in the past or their little tendencies that you thought were incidental. Like my husband, Bryan's, love for musicals and all things Broadway. Now, after the "incident," I see that as a sign. A sign that one day I would return home early from my graveyard shift because of a nagging headache and find my big, strapping, 6'4" husband stark naked and in the throes of passion with none other than one of our church's deacons. Maybe, if I'd paid closer attention to those tendencies, it wouldn't have come as such a shock to me. Maybe I would've been better prepared. But honestly, when you've been with a man for years, given him two sons, and believed that he loved you unconditionally, how can anything prepare you for that? Is preparation even a possibility?

That night, I walked into my home, a home we had worked hard to purchase. We were even ahead on the payments. At any rate, I walked into the house, my head throbbing, and the only thought in my mind was of taking an Aleve and then crawling into bed next to my man. That was it. I ascended the stairs slowly, because with each step, my headache seemed to intensify. I checked on my boys, first, to make sure they were asleep, because while Bryan was a good dad, he could be a little lackadaisical when it came to discipline, and it wasn't uncommon for him to allow them to stay up past their bedtime, regardless as to whether or not it was a school night. They were both fast asleep with the covers pulled over them and the night light illuminating one corner of their shared bedroom. I smiled as I turned and left their room, quietly closing the door behind me.

I slowly walked further down the hallway to the bedroom I shared with the love of my life, heard a strange sound, and stopped in my tracks. I wondered where the sound was coming from. But, almost instantly, my house was silent again—no sounds could be heard except for my own breathing. Then, there it was again. A grunt. A soft grunt, and it came from my husband; I was sure of that. After all the years we'd been together through courtship and marriage, I knew his voice, and I knew that grunt. It was a grunt I'd heard many times when we were making love. It was his signature, "Baby, this is good to me," grunt.

Before I realized what I was doing, I ran the short distance to my bedroom door. I ran right into it and, using the full force of all one hundred and sixty-seven pounds of my weight, busted it open and fell to the floor. A lot of thoughts ran through my mind, like how much of that heifer's hair I was going to pull out of her head, or how I was going to kick my husband in the groin and then put his dirty, lowdown, cheating tail out of my house, hopefully in nothing more than his Sean John boxer briefs. But as I sat up and tried to steady my dizzy head, the sight before me was almost more than I could believe. As a matter of fact, I blinked a few times to be sure I wasn't hallucinating. I surmised that maybe I was having visions as a side effect of the headache, like the aura that sometimes precedes a migraine. Because surely my eyes were playing a trick on me. Surely to God in Heaven I was not seeing what I thought I was seeing.

I was speechless for a second. My mind couldn't seem to formulate a single thought, and my mouth wouldn't have been able to convey it even if my mind had been functioning correctly. Lying there beneath my husband was Lamar Parker—our church's newest deacon, a handsome young man with a young wife and a young baby. There he was, the handsome Deacon Lamar Parker, naked, lying on his back *under* my husband. I didn't know what to do or how to react. I was so ashamed, but not of Bryan or Lamar. I was ashamed of myself for being so stupid and blind to the fact that my husband was gay.

My husband was gay.

Mine.

My husband.

He was *gay*.

As Lamar quickly climbed out of my bed, he wore a worried look on his face. He was talking, possibly saying something to me. I wasn't sure, because the only thing I could really hear was my own heartbeat and my own breathing, which were both unusually loud and rapid. I watched him pull on his underwear and pants, grab his shoes and shirt, and leave our bedroom. Then Bryan turned toward the door. There stood our oldest son, Derek, wide-eyed, probably wondering why a scantily clad man from our church had just rushed out of the bedroom, or why his dad was standing there wearing nothing but a condom, or why I was sitting on the floor in a daze. I wished I could've provided some form of comfort to my son, some semblance of solace, or at least a half-decent explanation, but I couldn't. I had no idea what was going on. I had not a clue why my husband, his father, was just having sex with a man.

Bryan wrapped a sheet around his body and ushered our ten-year-old son out of the room. When he returned, he closed the door behind him. "Carla, baby, let me explain," he said. He sounded like he was at the bottom of a well and his words were partially being soaked up by the water.

I shook my head and felt tears coursing down my face. I'm not a crying type of person—never have been. I pride myself on my strength and being able to take things as they come, but the things that *can* bring tears to my eyes are confusion and frustration, and at that moment, I was *very* confused and *extremely* frustrated. I just did not understand what was going on. I couldn't wrap my mind around the scene I had just, moments earlier, walked in on. I just could not.

I stood to my feet on shaky legs and took a second to steady myself. I wanted to sit down, but the thought of sitting on the bed made me heave. A mixture of the two men's colognes polluted the air of my bedroom and permeated my nose, adding to my nausea. I took a chance and walked over to the bathroom and sat on the side of the tub. Bryan followed me. "Are you okay?"

Well, that was about the dumbest question he could've asked at that moment. "What do you think, Bryan?" I asked, relieved that both my brain and mouth were once again working. "Pretend you're me. You come home from work early, because you have a headache, and then you walk in on your husband in bed with a *man*—naked and going at it. Now, tell me, would *you* be okay?"

He kneeled in front of me, his eyes wet and shiny with tears. One look at him, and I believed he was truly sorry. Maybe he was just sorry that he was caught, but I could tell this wasn't an act. He was genuinely sorry.

"I didn't mean for this to happen, baby. It's just that—"

I stared at him, at his full lips, at his handsome face and his strong body—the body that had always made me feel protected and safe—and I said, "Get out."

"Carla, listen. This will never happen again. I was just experimenting. I've got it out of my system now."

I stood on my unreliable legs. "Get out, Bryan. Pack a bag and leave." My voice was steady, but my heart was still racing, and my head felt like it was going to explode.

He stood to face me. "Let's just sleep on it and talk some more in the morning. Don't do this."

That was it. That was my breaking point. I flew into a rage and began pounding his muscular chest with my fists. He grabbed my arms, but somehow, I wrestled free from his grip. Then I slapped him with all of my might. "Get out of my house!" I screamed. "Right now!"

He relented, backed out of the bathroom, and a few minutes later, left our house carrying a packed suitcase. That was four years ago. Since then, I'd moved to St. Louis and back home. I'd tried unsuccessfully to sex my misery away, hoping that connecting with someone sexually would be a balm to a wound that was as deep as it was wide. Then reality hit. No matter how many men I slept with, it didn't, wouldn't, and couldn't change the fact that my husband had slept with a man, in my bed, in my home, just feet away from my sleeping sons. It couldn't change the fact that, despite possessing what I'd always been told was a pretty face and an hourglass figure, I lacked what he truly wanted in a partner.

We'd tried to reconcile; that didn't work. We still hadn't divorced, though. Evidently, neither one of us really wanted our marriage to end. So I found myself trying to make some sense of my life while attempting to raise two sons, one of which had just turned fourteen and was full of enough hormones and anger to fuel a team of professional wrestlers.

I'd moved, unable to stand even walking by that bedroom. Bryan lived in the house with the boys when it was his week to keep them. I lived in an apartment across town. I'd stopped attending church long ago—too ashamed and too disgusted with the down-low deacon who still graced the deacon's bench every Sunday, because no one knew the truth. And I certainly wasn't going to reveal it and solidify my own shame.

And so, my life consisted of phone calls to and from my bestie, Marli, visiting her and her new family in St. Louis from time to time, working, and taking care of my boys. Oh, and trying not to devise plans to kill Bryan. I hated to admit it, but four years later, I still hadn't forgiven him.

Sometimes, I even wondered what I ever saw in Bryan Maurice Foster. Then I'd quickly remember that he was tall, caramel-skinned, and handsome. I'd remember us holding hands in the early days, how his skin would contrast with my darker skin. How his big arms felt around my small body. How he'd wrap his arm around my waist and rest his hand on my wide hip when we stood side-by-side. I'd remember how tender he always was in the bedroom. I'd once been madly in love with him and had trusted him implicitly. He'd destroyed all of that.

2
"Like A Dream"

I reclined on my sofa and dialed Marli's number. I missed my friend so much sometimes. I was glad she was only a phone call away.

She answered after a couple of rings. "Hey, girl! What's up?"

"Hey, I'm good. How are the Kings?"

"We Kings are wonderful. The twins are a handful, as usual. And Chris has the nerve to want more kids! I told him he was crazy."

I laughed. "Y'all do make some pretty babies, though. Shoot, girl, if I was you, I'd give that man as many babies as he wants. Y'all can afford a nanny for each kid."

"Um, I don't want a nanny raising my kids. You wouldn't want that, either."

"Yeah, I hear you. There aren't too many people I trust with my boys."

"Yeah, so, what's been going on with you?"

I smiled. I knew where she was going with the conversation. "Nothing. Work."

"Met anyone interesting, lately?"

I sighed. "Nope. Not trying to meet anyone, either."

"Look, I know you took a vow of chastity after you moved back home, but you can still date, Carla. It's been years, and you and Bryan are not even trying to get back together anymore. I don't know why y'all are still married."

"I didn't take a vow of chastity. I'm just not having sex anymore. I'm over men, Marli. I'm done. And we're still married, because neither one of us wants a divorce."

"You're thirty-seven. So you're never going to be with another man? Really?"

"Girl, I was with enough men back in St. Louis to last me a lifetime. Believe me, I'll be fine."

"Don't you get lonely, Carla? I know I did before Chris."

I held the phone. I wasn't ready to admit that. Not even to my best friend.

"Look," Marli continued. "I'm happy for the first time in my whole life. I just want you to be happy, too."

I cleared my throat. "I already had my happy. I used to be happy with Bryan. I don't think I could ever be that happy again. I'm fine alone."

She sighed into the phone. "I'll leave it alone. But I'm praying for you."

"I appreciate that. So when are you gonna send me some more pictures of the prince and princess?"

The rest of the conversation was light, with Marli gushing about her wonderful husband and her good life. I wasn't mad at her. I liked hearing about her life, and I loved hearing the smile in her voice. If anyone on the planet deserved happiness, it was her. Marli's life had been sad story after sad story for a long time. It was almost as if our lives were reversed. While my marriage was going well, she was being cheated on, getting a divorce, and having to raise her child alone, all while dealing with crazy parents. At the same time, I was living the life with Bryan—in love, great kids, no money woes.

My parents had always been supportive, and I had a brother who would go to war for me at the drop of a hat. I was happy for years, content with my life as it was, madly in love with the high school quarterback who went to college and became a dentist. I had my happy until Bryan decided to mess it all up. No, I was doing the right thing. No more men. There was no way I could ever be that happy again. There was no way I could trust another man. I would just stay married to Bryan, but live on my own. Things were fine this way.

***

I woke up in the middle of the night after a bad dream. I dreamt that a big, black dog was chasing me through my house—the house I once shared with Bryan. The dream had been so real that I could still hear the growling and snarling echoing in my head after I woke up. I sat up in bed and tried to remember what my mama used to say about dreams, about what a dog chasing you meant. Mama was always an old soul. She could interpret dreams and see things in people just by looking at them. She could read you a mile away, see you coming before you arrived. I lost count of the number of times I wanted to ask her why she didn't warn me about Bryan's duplicity, because I knew she knew. She always did.

If it hadn't been after midnight, I would have called and asked her to interpret the dream for me, but I decided to wait. Calling at that hour would wake up the whole house—Mama, Daddy, and Grandma Tooley. And the call would probably scare my folks to death. No, it would just have to wait.

The next morning, I got out of bed after having lain there awake for most of the night. I shuffled into my kitchen, made an oversized mug of coffee, and carried it back to my bedroom, where I sat on the side of my bed and dialed my parents' number. Mama and Daddy, Claudie and Felicia Tooley, had grown up together, had loved each other since they learned what love was, and had been married for thirty-nine years. They were the kind of couple every couple strove to be like. You never saw one without the other. Daddy still opened doors for Mama. Mama still ironed his underwear and the sheets. They loved and respected each other, and I'd tried to model what they had in my marriage with Bryan. Of course, I'd failed.

Mama answered the phone with, "Good morning, Carla Sue."

I smiled. "Good morning, Mama. I didn't wake you, did I?"

"Girl, you know I wake up with the chickens. Getting your daddy's breakfast ready before he heads to work, right now. Something on your mind? You don't usually call this early in the morning."

"Tell Daddy I said to have a good day." My daddy was a principal at one of the local high schools.

"I will."

"How's Grandma Tooley?"

"Demented and mean as ever. She decided she ain't getting out of bed this morning, so I'ma have to serve her breakfast in bed. Lord knows she ain't easy to take care of, but I try to remember better days. Before this dementia kicked in, she was an angel to me."

"Yes, ma'am, I remember that."

"Hold on a minute."

The next voice I heard was my father's authoritative, baritone voice. "Hey, Carla Sue. Good to hear your voice this morning. But since you're just across town, you could've joined us for breakfast, you know?"

I sighed quietly. I hadn't visited my parents in a long time. I was trying to deal with life as it was, and seeing them together, though I loved them so, was hard for me. That was the same reason I didn't visit Marli too often. "I'll be by soon, Daddy."

"I'ma hold you to that. Bye, baby. Here's your mama."

"Hey, let me eat with your daddy, and I'll call you back," Mama said.

"Okay."

I sat there and drank the rest of my coffee, thinking to myself that I'd be glad when Bryan brought the boys back the next day. It was too quiet in that apartment without them. Just as that thought skated through my mind, Mama called me back.

"You had a dream. Go on and tell me about it," she said.

"How you know that's what it is?" I asked, not at all surprised that she knew.

"Girl, please. You are not a morning person. Never have been. That's why you work nights. I know you've got to be calling this early in the morning for a reason. What was the dream about?"

"A big, mean dog was chasing me through me and Bryan's house."

"Hmm," she said.

I didn't speak. I just held the phone and waited for more. She was silent a few seconds longer before she spoke. "That dog can be a couple of things. It could be a demon. I wouldn't be surprised if it was since you stopped going to church. You get too far away from God, and evil will not only chase you, it'll overtake you. Or... it could be a problem or an issue you're running away from. The fact that it was chasing you through the house tells me it's probably the latter. You and Bryan been in limbo too long—married, but separated. It's time for y'all to get it together or wrap things up."

I had a feeling she'd been wanting to tell me these things for a while, and the dream had finally given her the opportunity to get it off of her chest. "Okay, thank you, Mama."

"Well, let me tend to Mrs. Tooley. Pray, Carla Sue. And get yourself together for those boys' sake."

"Yes, ma'am."

"All right, baby. I love you. Talk to you later."

"Love you, too."

3
"Goodbye Game"

I felt the same way I always felt on Sunday evenings when I heard the knock at the door—elated that my boys were home, anxious at the thought of seeing Bryan again. I took a deep breath before opening the door. Patrick fell into me, hugging me tightly. Derek wore his usual, sour expression and walked past me while uttering an unenthusiastic, "Hey, Mama."

I squeezed Patrick in my arms. "Hey, Derek. Hey, Patrick. I missed you guys so much."

"I missed you, too, Mama," Patrick said as he looked up at me and smiled. He was growing so fast. Though he was only eleven, he was barely an inch or so shorter than my 5'5". As I hugged him, my eyes drifted over to Bryan, who seemed to look better every time I laid eyes on him. My heart thudded in my chest. I hated how seeing him made me feel. I hated being so heartbroken even after four years.

Bryan gave me a little smile. "Um, hey," he said softly.

"Hey." I ran my hand over Patrick's head. "Baby, can you go to your room? I need to talk to Daddy for a second."

Patrick nodded. "Okay. See you later, Daddy."

After Patrick left, Bryan and I stood there and faced each other in awkward silence for a full minute before I decided to invite him in. He sat on the loveseat; I sat on the sofa, and then we were surrounded by even more silence. Finally, I said, "Um, we need to talk. I mean, not now, with the boys around, but we need to talk about... us."

He nodded. His eyes lit up a little. "Okay, well, you can come by the office tomorrow if you want. I don't see my first patient until 10:00 A.M. Can you come before then?"

"Um, sure. I'll just drop by after I take the boys to school."

"Good. See you then."

***

I was so nervous when I walked into Bryan's office and approached the receptionist, you would've thought I was getting ready to testify in court. The short wait seemed to stretch on for hours. I was anxious—ready to take my mother's advice and wrap things up. I was ready to move on with my life, and I definitely didn't want to have that dream again.

Bryan came out into the waiting area and escorted me to his office. As I sat in a chair in front of his desk, I eyed the family portraits that still hung on his wall as if nothing had happened between us, as if he hadn't betrayed me, broken my heart, and left me in shambles. I crossed my blue jean-covered legs and took a deep breath. "Um, so, I think we should go ahead with a divorce," I said as he sat down in his black, leather executive chair.

He shook his head. "I don't agree. There's still love between us. I still love you. We just need more time."

I uncrossed my legs and leaned forward. "It's been four years, Bryan, and I still feel the same. That's not going to change."

He stood, walked around the desk, and squatted in front of me. "I know you still love me. I can see it in your eyes right now. I *know* you love me."

I sighed. "Bryan—"

"I made a huge mistake. I messed up. I let curiosity get the best of me, and I messed up. But I love you, Carla. *I love you.*"

My head tightened. "*Curiosity?* You had sexual relations with another person, *a man*, in our bed, with our boys in the same house! You call that curiosity?!"

Bryan grabbed both of my hands and squeezed them. "I am so sorry, baby. What you're saying? It's all true. I'm *worthless*. I ain't worth the spit it takes to cuss me. But I love you. I love you and my sons more than anything in this world. I'm not divorcing you. I don't care if it takes until we're a hundred years old, I'm not going to give up. I'll wait however long it takes for you to forgive me."

"I can't forgive you, Bryan. I've tried. I really have. I just can't do it."

"Do you love me, Carla?"

I shook my head. "That doesn't matter."

"Yeah, it does. If you can look me in the eye and tell me that you don't love me, I'll file for divorce today, give you everything you want. Just say it."

"I don't love you," I said without hesitation, my eyes glued to his.

"You're lying."

"You didn't say it had to be the truth."

He reached up and softly kissed my cheek. "I love you, Carla Sue Foster. I love you with everything that I am. I love you, and I'm sorry. I can't let you go, baby." He stood and pulled me to my feet. He wrapped his arms around me and kissed my cheek again, then my neck, then my lips. He rubbed his hands up and down my body. His touch was so familiar, and though I wished otherwise, my body welcomed it. Every caress, every kiss, every murmur from his lips was like paradise to me. I'd missed him. I'd missed being touched like that *period*. It had been a long, *long* time since I'd been with a man. So when he pulled me to the floor and began to pull my jeans off of me, I didn't protest.

It felt weird being with Bryan in that way again—weird, but good. We hadn't made love since before I caught him with the good deacon. Even during the short period of time of our attempted reconciliation, we never took it that far. We spent time together as a family, even fell asleep on the couch together a couple of times, but we never had sex. At the time, I couldn't get the horrible image I walked in on that night out of my head. But this time, as we made love in his office, the images didn't return to my mind. Maybe, I was over it all. Maybe, enough time had passed that we really could be together again.

I felt pretty good as I left his office with the sensation of his kisses still dancing on my skin. I could almost feel his touch as I climbed into my car. I smiled all the way home.

The next few days brought more of the same. I met Bryan at his office for lunch, and instead of eating, we made love. He even dropped by my place a couple of times after the boys had gone to bed. I enjoyed our time together, our stolen moments. It almost felt like we were young again, back when we were madly in love and couldn't get enough of each other. Back then, we would sneak behind my parents' back to make out. It was a miracle I didn't get pregnant until after we were married, because we were certainly reckless back then.

Our rekindled romance lifted my spirits and made me believe that maybe what we had was worth fighting for. I even told Bryan that we could start talking about reconciling. When I called and told Marli what was going on, she was happy for me, of course. She just wanted me to be happy, and anyone could hear the lift in my mood in my voice. And as a sort of confirmation, the dog chasing dream had not returned. It was right for us to be together again. I truly believed that. I felt it, too. My heart felt so much lighter.

***

Two months into our reconciliation courtship, I was feeling like a new woman. Not one day had gone by that I didn't see my husband or feel his loving touch. If we weren't together physically, we were on the phone, cooing loving words to each other. Plans were in place for me to move back into the home that had once been my pride and joy. The only thing left to do was to tell the boys. That was the one step that I'd been inexplicably hesitant to take. I had no idea why, but I'd been putting it off despite the fact that I was eager to be with Bryan again, wholly.

I was to meet Bryan for lunch that day. I was really looking forward to it, because I knew we'd be doing very little eating. I was wearing a big smile as I approached the receptionist. That smile didn't fade when I took a seat in the waiting area and began to thumb through a magazine. I was deeply engrossed in the latest issue of *O Magazine* when I saw him. Well, actually, I *smelled* him first. The scent of his cologne was unmistakable. It was a scent I'd *never* forget. It had been engrained into my very psyche.

As I lifted my eyes to follow his stride through the waiting area, my heart skipped. There could've been several logical reasons for his presence at that office. It was a huge dental practice with three dentists in residence. He could've been there for something as routine as a cleaning. He could've been there to see either of the other two very capable dentists and not Bryan. There was no good reason for me to believe he was there to see my husband, but I knew that was exactly why he was there.

Before I realized what I was doing, I was on my feet, exiting through the glass door with my husband's name etched on it, *Bryan Foster, DDS*. I'd followed Lamar Parker all the way to his car before he noticed me. He gave me a startled look and just stood there. We stared at each other for a while before he unlocked his car door and climbed inside, then drove off without a word. When I turned around to head back to the office to—I have no idea what I was going to do—but when I turned around, Bryan was standing outside the door with his nice, white dentist's coat on. He was staring at me with horror on his face. My first instinct was to run toward his Lexus SUV and key it up, then run up to him and key *him* up. But I couldn't move a muscle. My feet were glued to the pavement beneath them.

Noticing my state of paralysis, Bryan approached me. "I know how that looked, but I am telling you, *nothing is going on*. I haven't seen him since that night, Carla. I swear to God, nothing is going on."

I raised my burdened eyes to meet his gaze. "Why was he here?"

"He wanted to talk."

"About what?"

"He... he wanted to hook up again, but I told him *no way*. I told him what happened between us was a onetime mistake."

I sighed as I leaned against someone's car. All of the adrenaline that had propelled me from my seat in the waiting room out into that parking lot was gone, and now I felt like a deflated balloon. I was too exhausted from sheer shock and disappointment to scream or rage at him. "Why would he approach you out of the blue four years after the one and only time you two were together?"

He stood there for a full thirty seconds with a dumbfounded look on his face. "I... I don't know."

"You've been lying to me. You never stopped seeing him. You just didn't expect us to cross paths."

"Carla, baby—"

I gripped my throbbing head. "I just wish you were man enough to tell me the truth. If you want to be with him, if you're gay, just tell the truth, and stop playing with me."

"I'm not gay! Maybe he got wind of the fact that we're reconciling and is trying to purposely sabotage us. I don't know why he showed up today, but I know I'm not gay. I don't want him. I want my family. I want *you*." He reached for me, and I snatched away.

"I was fooling myself, thinking this would work. He'll always be around, or at least the thought of him will. I can't get over this. I can *never* get over this." I turned to leave, and Bryan grasped my arm. "Let me go. You don't want me to cause a scene, but best believe, I will."

He released me, and I stumbled to my car and slid into the driver's seat. I sat there for more than an hour, replaying that afternoon's events in my head. I was glad the boys were spending the week with Bryan, because I honestly was in no mental state to be around them. When I finally composed myself enough to drive home, I walked into my apartment and curled up on my couch. I didn't eat or answer the phone for two whole days. I was too numb to do anything but lie there day after day and sleepless night after sleepless night and wonder what I had done to deserve being hurt all over again.

4

"Mine"

I wasn't sure how I was going to be able to face Bryan when it was time for him to bring the boys back home, because he had truly disgusted me. But after a few days of being stuck in a depression, I finally snapped out of it. I told myself that this was my own fault and that I should have stuck with my first mind. I should have stuck to my guns about the divorce instead of letting him sex me into changing my mind. From the moment I let him undress me in his office, I began thinking with my lady parts rather than my head. *No more.* We were done. I wasn't giving him another chance to humiliate me. He wasn't going to get another shot at breaking my heart.

I got up that morning and pulled myself together. I showered and combed my hair for the first time in a week. I made up my face and treated myself to a manicure. I cooked a big dinner for my boys instead of ordering a pizza like I usually did. I even baked some cookies. My final task was emailing Hilda Stephens, a high school classmate who was a lawyer. I was determined to get the ball rolling on the divorce. I wasn't going to waste another year as Bryan Foster's wife.

He brought the boys home around five that evening, as usual. He wore a sheepish expression on his face when I opened the door. But as he took in my appearance, his eyes widened. I didn't even bother to speak to him. I welcomed my sons home and shut the door in Bryan's face. He called off and on all night, but I didn't answer.

When I finally climbed into bed, I switched my cell phone's ringer to off.

Around 1:00 A.M., I was awakened by a knock at the door. My first thought was not to answer it at all as I remembered my mother's words: "Anyone out after midnight ain't up to no good." But whoever it was wouldn't stop knocking, and I didn't want to run the risk of them waking the boys up. I walked to the door in my night shirt and jogging pants and checked the peep hole. My curiosity transformed into irritation when I saw Bryan standing on the other side of the door.

"Bryan? What are you doing here at this time of the morning? You're gonna wake the whole building up."

"Let me in, Carla," he said, sounding upset. "I need to talk to you."

"Bryan, we ain't got nothing to talk about at one in the morning. Go home."

"You got someone in there you don't want me to see?"

I rolled my eyes. "Go home."

"You're all fixed up, and I could smell the food you cooked, and you wouldn't answer the phone all damn night. You better not have another man in there with my sons."

"Don't worry, you already did that. No sense in me repeating your sins."

"That was a low blow. Let me in, Carla."

"No. I'm going back to bed. You need to go home and stop beating on my door before someone calls the police."

I left him at the door. He kept knocking for a while, and then I guess a little of his common sense kicked in, and he stopped. When Patrick climbed into bed with me about thirty minutes later, I thought Bryan had woken him up, but no, he just missed me. I was happy to cuddle up with my baby boy.

***

The next morning, I dropped my boys off at school and headed back home. I had work that night, so I called to be sure my babysitter—my cousin, LaDonna—could still stay with the boys as she usually did. Derek was fourteen, but I just wasn't comfortable leaving him and Patrick alone at night for the twelve hours I would be at work. After a little light conversation with LaDonna, I fixed myself a bowl of cereal and settled down in front of the TV for my daily dose of mindless entertainment. Judge Mathis was on, handing out his brand of justice. Around noon, there was a knock at my door. I had no idea who it could be, other than my mother. It had been so long since I'd visited my parents, I wouldn't have been surprised if she was standing at my door with Grandma Tooley in tow. When I checked the peephole, I sighed.

"Why aren't you at work? Don't you have some teeth to pull? Lovers to meet?" I said.

"Baby, let me in," Bryan said, sounding even more desperate than he had the night before.

"Why?" I said with a smirk. A part of me was enjoying myself, enjoying the fact that he was upset. Part of me wanted him to hurt at least half as much as he'd hurt me.

"I need to talk to you. Let me in."

I unlocked the door so that I could watch him grovel, but I was determined that the end result would be the same. We were not reconciling. I was keeping my appointment with Hilda Stephens. We were getting divorced, and that was final.

He followed me into the living room and sat so close to me that our thighs touched. I moved over a little. He moved even closer.

"What do you want to talk about, Bryan?"

"We've got to work this out. We've *got* to."

I sighed. "We can't. You can't even tell me the truth."

"I've been truthful, Carla. I have not been unfaithful to you since that night. That's the truth."

"I don't believe you. And that's all that matters. I know what I saw at your office, the look on Lamar's face. Just tell the truth. If you're gay, or bi, or whatever, I won't hold it against you. As a matter of fact, I'll respect you more for admitting it."

"I'm not gay *or* bi!" he shouted. "Why can't you believe me?!"

I frowned. "Probably because I caught you having sex with a *man*! Then I saw *the same man* sneaking out of your freakin' office four years later!"

He fell to his knees and wrapped his arms tightly around me. "Baby, please. I can't take this anymore. Last night, I felt like I was gonna die. All I could think about was you being with someone else. I couldn't take that. I love you so much."

I pushed against him. "Yeah, well, been there, done that several times already."

"What? You've been unfaithful to me?" He actually looked shocked.

"That would be an understatement," I mumbled, recollecting my many St. Louis indiscretions.

"What?"

I raised my eyebrows and my voice. "We've been separated for *four years*, Bryan... so, yeah, I have been *very* unfaithful."

"Doesn't matter. I deserved it."

"Look, I've made an appointment with a lawyer. We can't go on like this. I think we should end things. As a matter of fact, I'm *sure* we should. Now let me go."

He tightened his hold on me. "I can't let you go. I *won't* let you go."

"Bryan—"

He covered my mouth with his as I struggled to break free from him.

"Stop!" I grunted against his mouth.

"*No,*" he said once our lips parted.

I pushed harder against him. He, in turn, held me tighter. "For real, Bryan, let me go."

He nuzzled my neck. "No."

"Bryan—"

He grabbed my face so tightly; his manicured fingernails dug into the flesh of my cheeks. "You're my wife. You can't deny me of what's mine."

"What?" I stared at him. He didn't look or even sound like himself. I felt my heart begin to thunder in my chest. Every nerve in my body was on edge. "Bryan, I haven't really been your wife in a long time. You know that."

He let go of my face and pressed a hard kiss against my lips—so hard that my teeth nearly cut into the inside of my mouth. Then he took his hand and gripped my neck while clutching my shirt with his other hand, ripping it. "You'll always be my wife. Till death do us part, remember?" he whispered harshly.

"What's wrong with you? Bryan..." I croaked. "Bryan, *please*."

He didn't hear me, or maybe he did and just didn't care. He kept one hand wrapped around my neck as he tugged my pants down over my hips with the other. When he let me go to unzip his pants, I decided to take a chance. I kicked my pants off, jumped up, and ran to my bedroom, locking the door behind me. I'd left my phone in the living room, so I couldn't call for help. I sat on the side of my bed, trembling. I jumped to my feet when I heard the loud thud on the bedroom door. I knew right away that he wasn't knocking. He was trying to kick the door in. I ran to my nightstand and grabbed the kitchen knife that I kept in the drawer for protection. When the door busted in, I shrieked and wondered where the hell the neighbors were. There was no way I could hear that much commotion and not call the police. Surely someone would call. *Surely*.

I raised the knife as I turned to face him. He smiled at me. "What you gonna do with that?" he asked.

"Stay back," I said, my voice unsteady.

He moved closer. I held the knife out toward him, and before I realized what was happening, he'd grabbed my arm and squeezed it so tightly that I dropped the knife. My heart galloped. My throat went dry. I reached up and scratched his face with my free hand. What he did next, I never thought he'd do. It was something he'd never done before. *He punched me.* He punched me so hard that I actually fell to the floor, blood spilling from my nose. He yanked his pants down, and the next thing I knew, he was on the floor, too, on top of me, pinning me down.

"Bryan, please don't do this. Please, please, *please!*"

Unmoved by my desperate pleas, he covered my mouth with one hand, held down both my wrists with the other, forced my legs open with his knees, and there on my bedroom floor, my husband of more than fifteen years raped me.

He raped me.

5
"Get Through the Night"

I lay there beneath his heavy, sleeping body—afraid to move. Unrelenting tears flowed from my eyes into my ears as I stared at the ceiling, my throat sore from screaming into the palm of his hand—begging him to stop. I was trying to understand what had happened, trying to figure out who the man on top of me was. Bryan had never been a violent man. He'd never raised a hand to me before. He'd barely ever even raised his voice. I usually won all of our arguments, because he wasn't very confrontational at all. That's how we'd managed to be separated for so long. He just never made a big fuss about it. But as I lay there, I realized that what he'd just done must've been something he was always capable of. It was always there inside of him. He'd been too good at doing it, at hurting me.

As I slowly tried to wriggle my body from underneath his, his head snapped up and he looked at me, into my eyes. I stared back at him and froze. My heart jumped in my chest. Was he going to rape me again?

"Where are you going?" he asked softly.

"I-I-I-I need to get dressed so I-I can pick the boys up from school," I whispered.

He shook his head. "I'll get 'em. I know you're probably tired." He gently kissed me, lifted his weight off of me, and sprang to his feet. He left my bedroom, and I slowly sat up. My nose stung and my head spun. He walked back into the bedroom and threw my clothes at me. Then he sat at the foot of the bed and put his pants back on.

"I'll be right back," he said in his normal voice. "You better get cleaned up."

I nodded.

After he left, I stumbled to the bathroom and inspected myself in the mirror. I stared at the crusted blood under my nose, at the bruises on my neck and wrists, where Bryan had pinned me down. I winced as the soreness between my legs seemed to intensify with every beat of my heart.

I ran a tub full of steamy, hot water and slowly lowered myself into it. I washed the blood from my face and submerged my head in the water. I held my breath and closed my eyes and tried to shut my mind off. I told myself that it had been a dream, a nightmare. What happened didn't really happen. It couldn't have. That was it. None of it was real. None of it happened.

I climbed out of the tub, and by the time I'd walked back into my bedroom and toweled off, I could hear my sons' happy voices coming from the living room. I hadn't left the bedroom to lock the front door, so I assumed they'd let themselves in. Then I heard Bryan's voice, and every muscle in my body went as stiff as a corpse in rigor mortis. I stood there, stark naked, my eyes darting to the closed bedroom door that would no longer lock. I quickly ducked back into the bathroom and locked myself inside. I was sitting on the toilet, a trembling mess, when I heard the light knock at the door. And as light and unthreatening a knock as it was, it still startled me.

"Carla? You in there?" Bryan asked.

My eyes clouded, and my heart pounded. I couldn't speak.

The doorknob jiggled. "Carla?"

Salty tears raced over my cheeks into my open mouth. I clutched my stomach with one hand and covered my mouth with the other, to hold in my sobs.

"Look, I figured you wouldn't feel like cooking, so I got you and the boys a bucket of chicken and some sides. I would stay and eat with you guys, but I promised my mom I'd go by there and check her toilet. It's leaking or something. You know how she thinks I'm her personal Mr. Fix-it," he said with a chuckle.

I sucked in a breath and blew it out.

"You okay in there?"

I finally managed to say, "Yeah, I'm fine. Um... tell the boys I'll be out in a second."

"Okay. Love you. See you later."

I sat there for a long while, afraid that if I stepped outside of the safety of the bathroom, Bryan would be standing right outside the door, waiting on me. Waiting to hurt me again. When I heard another knock at the door, I gasped and stared at it.

"Mama, can we eat? I'm hungry." It was Derek.

I closed my eyes and breathed a sigh of relief. "Is your daddy gone?"

"Yes, ma'am. He *been* gone. Can we eat? Patrick is out here whining."

"Yeah, go ahead. And be sure to lock the front door."

"Okay."

I waited for him to leave before I opened the door and stepped into my bedroom. I pulled on a nightshirt and sat on the side of the bed and stared at the spot on the floor where Bryan attacked me. I sat there for more than an hour before I realized time was drawing near for me to go to work, but I knew I was in no condition to go. I walked over to the door, cracked it open, and called for Patrick. He came running down the hall with a big, greasy grin on his face. "Yes, Mama?!"

I smiled down at him despite the pain that was filling me to the brim.

Patrick frowned. "You got a nosebleed?"

I quickly covered my nose with my hand and could feel the warm blood oozing from it. "Yeah, I guess I do," I said, trying to make it sound like it was a regular, old nosebleed. "Can you bring me my cell phone from the living room?"

"Okay."

After he brought the phone to me, I stuffed tissue up my nose to stop the bleeding, then I called off work. I called my cousin to cancel her babysitting, too. Then I told the boys I wasn't feeling well, and I climbed into bed for the night.

***

I didn't sleep a wink that night, because every time I closed my eyes, I saw Bryan's face, felt his fist crunch against my nose, felt the pressure of his heavy body as he pinned me to the floor, saw the gold, cross necklace that swung from his neck like a pendulum as he violated me. I spent the entire night lying in my bed, wide awake, listening to the silence of my apartment. I didn't cry. I didn't make a sound. I just lay there and prayed for sleep to overtake me, but it never did.

The next morning, I felt like a zombie as I showered, dressed, and packed on makeup to cover the bruising on my neck and around my nose. I drove my boys to school, struggling to keep my heavy eyelids open as I weaved through the morning traffic. *Now, I'm sleepy?* I thought. After I dropped them off at their schools, I drove to a grocery store and parked on the lot. I couldn't go back home and risk Bryan forcing his way back into my apartment. I knew that he'd be hesitant to try anything like that with the boys around, but he'd know they were at school. I sat there for ten minutes before deciding to go to my parents' house.

I pulled my car into the driveway and walked around back to the kitchen door, where I was sure Mama was feeding Grandma Tooley or washing the morning's dishes. I knocked on the screen door and waited. About a second later, I heard my mother's voice.

"Who is it?"

"It's me, Mama."

The door slowly creaked open to reveal my beautiful mother, with her flawless, ebony skin. She smiled. "Well looka here. If it isn't my wayward daughter. Girl, you look tired. Come on in here."

I stepped into the warmth of my parents' home, which smelled of pork sausage and molasses. As my mother pulled me into a tight hug, I glanced over at the platter of food on the table. If I weren't so tired and my stomach not in knots, I would've gladly fixed myself a heaping plate of my mother's good cooking. But all I could think about was finding somewhere to lay my head.

"Sit down. Let me fix you a plate," she said.

I obeyed my mother, and after she sat the full plate of sausage, eggs, and biscuits drenched in molasses in front of me, I said grace and really tried to eat. But when Mama left the kitchen to check on my grandmother, I pushed the plate aside and rested my head on the table. Before I knew it, I was fast asleep. I nearly jumped straight up when Mama shook me awake.

"Girl, what is wrong with you? You jumped like the devil was touching you. If you're tired, you can lie down in the guest bedroom."

I nodded. "Yes, ma'am." I shuffled through the house I grew up in, to the room that was once mine, and fell into the bed and into a glorious, much-needed sleep.

This became my daily routine. I'd call in sick to work, lie awake all night, take my boys to school, and hide out at my parents' house in the day time and sleep. After a week of this, I couldn't believe that my mother hadn't given me the third degree about why I was suddenly visiting every day, but knowing my mother, she knew something was wrong. She probably knew that I didn't want to talk about it, as well. Bryan called every night, but I didn't answer the phone. Thankfully, he didn't drop by the house any of those nights, because I didn't want to have to make up a lie to tell my sons to explain why I didn't want their father in our home. But after a week of successfully dodging Bryan, my luck ran out. He found me at my parents' house.

I was lying in my old bed, fast asleep, when I felt someone gently shake my shoulder. I thought it was my mother telling me it was time to pick the boys up, so I kept my eyes closed and muttered, "Just a second, Ma. I'm getting up."

"It's not your mother. It's me."

Bryan's voice vibrated in my head, setting off alarms. My eyes popped open, and almost instantly, I scrambled out of the bed on the side opposite of where he stood. My heart was beating so fast, I don't see how it didn't stop altogether. "What are you doing here?" I asked as my eyes darted to the closed bedroom door.

"I've been trying to reach you for over a week. I even called your job looking for you. They told me you've been off sick. What's wrong?"

My eyes searched the room. There was a heavy, old lamp sitting on the night stand right next to me. If he tried anything, I was going to break it over his head.

"You can't talk? Got laryngitis or something?" he asked.

"I'm fine. Tired is all."

"You been too tired to talk to me?" He moved forward a little.

I reached for the lamp. "Stay back, Bryan."

"Stay back? Carla, what's wrong with you?"

My eyes widened. "What's wrong with me?! What's *wrong* with me?! Are you serious?!"

"Is this about the fight we had the other day? We made up in the end. I thought you'd be over that by now."

"We made up?! What are you talking about?"

He lowered his voice. "We had sex, remember?"

I stared at him. My entire body began to tremble. "That was not just *sex*," I said in a harsh whisper. "You hit me, and you pinned me down, and you *forced* me to have sex with you."

"*Forced* you?" he asked with a genuinely shocked look on his face.

"Yes!"

He shook his head. "Nah, you wanted it. I could tell."

I frowned. I could feel my head begin to throb. "You think I *wanted* you to bust my nose?"

"Okay, I guess I got a little rough. I just wanted you, baby. If I hurt you, I'm sorry."

"Rough? You *raped* me."

He frowned and actually looked a little confused. "A man can't rape his wife, Carla."

"I said, *no*. I fought you. You *took* it from me."

He shook his head again. "If I raped you, why am I not in jail? Why didn't you call the police?"

"Because—" I stopped. I had raised my voice. I lowered it and continued, "Because of the boys. I didn't want them to have to see you behind bars."

"I didn't rape you. I... I love you. I *made* love to you."

I clasped my shaky hands in front of me. "That wasn't love. That... that was—just leave me alone, Bryan."

"No. We need to talk. When are you moving back in?"

I stood there and stared at him and tried to figure out if he was really as oblivious as he sounded. The look in his eyes told me that he was. I moved toward the door. He moved to block me.

"*Get out of my way*," I said. "If you don't, I'm gonna scream bloody murder, and my mama is gonna call the police if she doesn't get my daddy's shotgun and blast you first. *Move*."

"Look, I just wanna talk to you. *I love you*. Don't let what happened ruin what we've been working so hard to put back together."

"What are you talking about? *You* are what happened! YOU! *You* cheated! *You* hurt me. You *keep* hurting me! You! It's all YOU!" I shouted.

"What's going on in here?" My mother asked as she slowly opened the door. "Mrs. Tooley just fell asleep. I don't need her to wake back up yet. Bryan, you said you needed to talk. Now, I don't appreciate you coming into my house yelling and screaming. You know I don't allow that kind of disrespect in my home."

"I'm sorry, Ms. Felicia, but I'm not the one in here yelling," Bryan said.

Mama turned to me. I could tell she was about to fuss, but she hesitated and let her eyes lock with mine. She stared at me for a moment and then turned back to Bryan. "Bryan, let me show you out."

He opened his mouth to protest, took one look at my mother's stern expression, and said, "Um, okay. Sorry to cause any trouble." He glanced at me. "I'll call you later, baby."

He left, and I felt my entire body relax. "Thank you, Mama."

Mama moved closer to me and rested her hand on my arm. "Carla, what's going on?"

I stared at the floor. "I told him I want a divorce, and he's not taking it too well."

"He hit you?"

I shook my head rather than verbalize my lie.

"You know I can see right through you. *Did he hit you?*"

"I don't wanna talk about it."

"If he hit you, you're right to divorce him."

I nodded. "I need to go now, Mama."

She reached for me, pulled me into a warm hug. "The next time he hits you, you call the police. Don't let him get away with it again," she whispered in my ear. She stepped back and held my face in her soft hands. "You hear me?"

I nodded and whispered, "Yes, ma'am."

6

"Fragile"

"Hey, were you busy?" I asked after Marli answered the phone.

"No, not at all. Been thinking about you. How's it going? I've been calling. You get my messages?"

"Yeah, I've been meaning to call before now. Things have just been... busy."

"Oh, I see. How are things? You moved back in with Bryan yet?"

I held the phone and stared out the windshield. I was sitting in my car on the parking lot at Patrick's school, too afraid to go back home, too ashamed to go back to my parents' house.

"Carla, what's going on? Things didn't work out?"

I felt my eyes well up, and for the first time since Bryan attacked me, I cried. My head throbbed as the tears fell. I sobbed pitifully into the phone.

"Carla! What's wrong? Do you need me to come there?" Marli sounded panicked, but I knew why. She knew I didn't cry easily, and for me to be crying this hard, something had to be terribly wrong.

"Carla, I'm coming. Me and Chris and the kids will be on the next plane to Arkansas. Do you hear me?"

I wanted to protest, to tell her not to come. I wanted to tell her that nothing was wrong and that I'd be fine. But most of all, I wanted all of that to be true. But I needed her. I needed my friend. I needed someone to hug me and hold my hand and tell me that I'd be okay. I needed someone to be strong for me, because all of my strength was gone. So I said, "Okay. Hurry."

I left the parking lot and got a room at a little fleabag motel across town just so I could get some sleep, because I was still unable to sleep at night. I set my phone to alarm in time for me to pick the boys up from school, and then I settled onto the lumpy mattress, pulling the natty cover over my body. I rested my head on the pillow, closed my eyes, and soon fell into a deep, dreamless sleep. My alarm went off at 2:45 P.M., and I got up, washed my face, and headed out the door.

The first thing I saw when I stepped onto the sidewalk in front of my room was Bryan's SUV parked a few doors down. My heart flipped as I ducked back inside the room. Had he followed me there? Was he somewhere lurking, waiting for me? I leaned against the shut door and told myself that I was being silly. Bryan wasn't the only person in town who drove that kind of vehicle. There were probably tons of them in town of the same make, model, and color. *Tons.* Bryan was a lot of things, but he was no stalker. But then again, he'd found me at my parents' house. Would it be that far-fetched for him to find me here? Either way, it was time to pick my boys up. I couldn't stay holed up in that motel room any longer. So I decided to make a run for it. I'd open the door and dash to my car. I would hit the button on my key fob and unlock it on the way. And that's exactly what I did.

I breathed a sigh of relief once I made it inside my car. I locked the doors and glanced around to see if there was any sign of Bryan. I didn't see him anywhere. I even checked the backseat just to be sure. I bought my SUV after we separated, so he shouldn't have had a key, and I was sure I'd locked my doors, but you never know. *Maybe it really isn't his car*, I thought. I took a deep breath, and as I put the car in reverse, noticed one of the room doors opening. I don't know why, but my first instinct was to put my car back in park and watch that door. When Bryan walked out of the room, I gasped. When Lamar Parker walked out behind him, I nearly choked on air. But when they embraced, I snatched my key out of the ignition, threw my door open, and stalked over to where they were. They were so locked up in that hug, they didn't even hear or see me walk up behind them. I pulled my phone from my pocket and began taking pictures like a paparazzo. I snapped about six pictures before Bryan turned around with a look of shock on his face.

"Carla? W... what're you doing here?!" he shrieked.

I gave him a smirk. "Catching your sorry tail in the act." I turned the phone around and showed him one of the pictures. He tried to grab it from me, but I snatched away from him and held the phone behind my back. "You'll hear from my lawyer. If you try to fight me on a divorce, if you don't agree to my terms, these pictures—yes, there's more than one—will go viral. I will post them all over the internet, and judging from how you keep denying the fact that you are gay, I assume you don't want these pictures seen by anyone."

"Carla—"

I held up a hand. "Save it. I don't want to look at your face ever again! From now on, drop the boys off and keep rolling." I turned to leave, and he grabbed my arm. "Let me go! Don't you ever put your hands on me again, or I will call the police so fast it'll make your head spin!" I shouted.

"Carla, *please* don't do this," Bryan pleaded.

I glanced at Lamar Parker, who stood behind Bryan with a bewildered look on his face. "Does your wife know?" I asked.

Lamar frowned. "What?"

"Does your wife know you're screwing my husband?"

Lamar didn't respond. He just stared at me like I was speaking a foreign language.

Bryan tightened his grip on my arm. "Carla, this is not what it looks like. Lamar wanted to talk. That's all we did. *Talk*."

"You usually do your talking in fleabag motel rooms?" I scoffed. "Open the door."

Bryan frowned. "What?"

"Open the door to that room. Let me see the bed. If it's intact, I'll believe you."

He loosened his grip on me, and a second later, let me go altogether.

I raised an eyebrow. "That's what I thought." And with that, I turned and left.

***

Marli and I had been friends since elementary school. We knew each other well. We had seen each other through some hard times and some good times. We'd shared our innermost secrets, dreams, and fears. When I revealed Bryan's infidelity to her, she'd not only been a listening ear, but a voice of reason as well, because I had truly gone off the deep end with my behavior. Her words at the time had reeled me back in to reality. I had done the same for her more than once. That's what friends do—provide a listening ear, a comforting voice, and sometimes, a good dose of reality.

When she arrived at my apartment, I was so glad to see her. Since marrying Chris and having the twins, she'd lost twenty pounds, and she looked *good*. She wore her natural hair cut close to her scalp and dyed blond. She reminded me of a much thicker, darker skinned, Amber Rose. And she had style for days, not to mention the rocks on her hands, but I guess being married to a rich man will do that for you. It seemed that Chris bought her a new piece of jewelry every month. He loved her—that was one thing I was sure of.

As we settled in my living room, I said, "I can't believe your hubby let you out of his sight."

She smiled. "His dad is running a revival, and Chris wanted to be there to support him. He'll be here in the morning with the twins. Plus, I thought we'd need some time just for you and me to talk."

"I'm sorry for dragging you away from your family."

"No problem, really. I'm just sorry it took me a whole day to get here."

I shook my head. "No, it's good you got here while the boys were at school. At least you're here with me now, and I'm not alone. I was tired of running and hiding."

Marli frowned. "What have you been hiding from?"

"Bryan."

The last thing I'd told her about me and Bryan was that I was getting ready to move back in with him. So I got her up to speed with everything that had occurred, all the way up to my confrontation with Bryan at the motel the day before. I even showed her the pictures in my phone. As Marli stared at one of the pictures, I said, "My life is a freakin' mess. I haven't had a decent night's sleep or been to work in forever, because I'm so tired I'm afraid I'll inadvertently kill a patient. Plus, I have absolutely no desire to go to work. But I'm scared to be here. My neighbors are so sorry, Bryan could break in here and attack me every day if he wanted to. They'll never help me."

"Can you afford to take a leave of absence from your job?" she asked.

"Yeah, I've got some money saved up. I probably need to do that before I get fired."

"If you see yourself running short, let me know. I know Chris won't mind if I help you."

I smiled at my friend. She was truly the best. "Thank you and him."

Marli hesitated, then looked me in the eye. "Why didn't you report Bryan for what he did to you?"

I shrugged. "I don't know. I think I was in shock at first. I really couldn't believe he'd done it. Then I started thinking about my boys. I didn't want to put them through anymore trauma."

"I understand that, but are you sure? You're just gonna let him get away with it?"

"It's what's best for my babies, and besides, I've watched enough *Law and Order: SVU* to know that it's too late. I've washed away all of the evidence. Plus, marital rape isn't easy to prove, especially in this case since we were about to reconcile. I'd just had sex with him a few days earlier. There's no way I'm putting myself or my sons through a trial that I'll probably lose."

"What're you gonna do? I mean, what's to stop him from doing it again?"

I shrugged. "I have no idea. But I've got these pictures, and maybe I can blackmail him or something. I just don't know, Marli. I don't know what I can do other than pray and hope he'll take heed of what I said and stay away from me."

"Maybe you should move somewhere a little safer, like a gated complex or something. I can help you if you need it."

I leaned forward and covered my face with my hands. "Maybe. I just can't think anymore. I'm so tired."

"Look, why don't you go lie down? We can figure out what to do later. I'm here for as long as you need me."

I looked up at my friend and sighed. "Thank you so much for being here."

"No problem. That's what friends are for. Get some rest."

I reached over and hugged her before leaving the living room, and as soon as I made it to my bedroom, I fell into bed and into a sound sleep.

7

"Be Ok"

Mere words cannot adequately explain how it felt to have my friend there with me. She cooked, she cleaned, she helped my boys with their homework, but most of all, she was there for me. I could walk around my home in peace, without fear of my husband showing up and kicking the door in and hurting me. I could breathe easier, sleep more peacefully, and after a week, I almost felt normal again. When her husband arrived with their kids, I was a little afraid that I'd start feeling down again. Like I said, Chris King was one man who truly loved his wife. There was barely a second that passed without him reaching for her hand or wrapping his arm around her shoulders or kissing her cheek. There was always a smile in his eyes when he looked at her, and I had never, *ever* seen her so happy. I was afraid seeing his love for her would remind me of the misery of my current situation, and it did a little, but by and large, having them there was truly a blessing to me.

And those twins of theirs were the cutest little kids, with their curly, sandy hair and blue eyes. Cute and active. I don't think they sat still for more than a few minutes at a time. But as much as I enjoyed their company, I knew I couldn't expect them to stay forever. They had a life in St. Louis. They'd offered for me to go home with them and stay for a while, and I actually thought about it but decided against it. I'd made a mess of things when I stayed there before, and Lord knows I didn't want to run into any of my former tryst partners. That would be too embarrassing. I was a different woman now—stronger in some ways, weaker in others. And the last thing I wanted or needed to do was to revisit that shameful part of my life. I decided that I would find a safer place to live in town, and after visiting my lawyer to start the divorce proceedings, I'd tell Marli it was okay for her to leave. Then I'd have to figure out how I was going to tell the boys about the divorce.

In the meantime, I had to work some things out in my mind. Even if I moved into a secure, gated community, I would still have to interact with Bryan as we exchanged custody. I sighed and closed my eyes as my friend combed my hair and greased my scalp. I glanced over at her husband, who was sitting on my sofa with a twin occupying each of his knees while he battled my oldest son at some video game. My baby, Patrick, was a very focused spectator.

"You are so lucky, Marli," I whispered.

"Hmm, I'm blessed," she said.

"Yes, you truly are."

"So are you, Carla."

I looked up at her with raised eyebrows, but I didn't reply. I knew what she meant, and by any standards, I *was* blessed. I had a roof over my head, a decent car, two healthy children, food in my kitchen, a nice savings account, and a good job waiting for me when I got my mind back together. But there was still that ache in my heart—the ache that I'd tried to fill with sex, mask with keeping busy, and just downright deny by ignoring it. It was still there. It had only intensified after Bryan assaulted me, and what bothered me more than anything was that I wasn't sure if it would ever go away. I wasn't sure if I'd ever feel better about my life.

Marli pushed against my shoulders. "Come with me."

I nodded and stood from my seat on the floor to my feet. I followed her through my apartment to my bedroom, where we sat side-by-side on my bed.

"I don't want to leave you here when we go back home, Carla. I'm worried about you."

I shook my head. "I'll be fine. Just go to the lawyer's with me, and I promise I'll be fine after that."

"Are you sure? I mean, when I got here, you weren't sleeping or eating or even handling your hygiene all that well, and judging from the condition of your hair, grooming wasn't that high on your list of priorities, either."

I sighed and dropped my head. "I was going through some things then. I'm better now."

She raised her eyebrows. "You were *raped*, Carla. And it affected you. You're not over it. You *know* you're not."

"I *have* to be over it. I have my boys to take care of."

"What are you gonna do after I leave? Are you going to be able to sleep or take a shower then?"

"I'm gonna find a new place with better security. We already discussed this."

She reached over and rested her hand on my shoulder. "You need to talk to someone about what happened. If you're not going to make Bryan pay for what he did, you need to at least help yourself."

I stood from the bed, my eyes glued to the spot on the bedroom floor where Bryan violated me. "I'm fine. I mean, it was partially my fault anyway."

Marli looked up at me with a frown. "How? What could you possibly have done to make him hit you and rape you?"

I gripped my head, which was beginning to ache. "I don't know. I guess I'm just trying to rationalize things, trying to make sense of what happened. I don't think he meant to hurt me. He's never laid a hand on me before. *Never*."

"Maybe he didn't mean to hurt you, but the fact is that he *did* hurt you. You can't rationalize what he did any more than you can rationalize his infidelity."

I slumped back down on the bed next to her. "I know." I looked over at her. "I know you're right about me getting some help, but I'm just not ready for that, Marli. It was hard for me to tell you, and you're my girl. I can't even imagine telling a stranger."

She nodded. "I understand, but it doesn't have to be a stranger. It can be your pastor. And you know, I went to therapy right after Chris and I got married. It's not as bad as it seems."

"You did, didn't you? I remember that. You said you were gonna get some professional help so you could be a good wife to him."

"Yes, and it really helped me. Look, you need to do the same, so you can be ready for your Mr. Right."

"I've said it before, and I'll say it again; I'm over men. I'm done. No more for me."

She tilted her head to the side and sighed. "I know you're hurt, but I just can't believe you're never gonna be with a man again. I just can't, and I definitely don't believe you're never gonna have sex again. *Not you*."

I rolled my eyes and my neck. "What does that mean—*not you*?"

"It means, I don't believe that *you*, of all people, can give up sex *permanently*. I know you have needs."

"Well, I've been praying for my vagina to go numb. Will you

pray with me?"

"No!"

"If you were really my friend, you would. I mean, what's wrong with praying for that? The Bible says ask and you shall receive, seek and you shall find—"

"Carla, I don't think that scripture applies to this situation."

"Well, I hope it does. The only way I'm gonna make it is with a numb vagina."

"That's what I'm saying. *You're not gonna make it.* I refuse to believe you are done with men for the rest of your life."

"Believe me. I'm not dating anymore, Marli. I'm done with men. My situation proves that what everyone's been saying is true. All of the good men are either married or gay or, as in my case, *both*."

"What about *my* case? Chris is a good man. Explain that."

"And he's married. You just proved my point for me."

She sighed loudly. "He wasn't married when I met him."

"Okay, then Chris King is the one and only exception to the rule."

"No. There are more men out there like him. I'm sure of that."

"Well, I'm not holding my breath, waiting for a tall, handsome, white man with black man tendencies and a ridiculous bank balance to sweep me off my feet."

She dropped her head. "Lord, you know what I mean. There's someone out there for you, but he'll never find you if you shut yourself off to the possibility of him even existing."

"Look, like I said, I was happy once. Now I'm not, and I don't ever expect to be again. I'm done discussing this. Now let's get back out there with your husband. He's a good man, but I don't know if he can handle all four of our kids alone."

She chuckled. "Yeah, I guess we should go rescue him." She stood from the bed and reached for my hand. "Come on, bestie."

I took her hand and pulled her into a hug. "Thank you for being here."

She squeezed me and said, "Where else would I be?" She backed away from me a little. "Will you at least think about seeing someone? Like I said, it doesn't have to be a therapist. You could talk to your pastor."

"I can't even tell you the last time I stepped foot in a church," I admitted.

She raised an eyebrow. "Don't you think that's part of the problem?"

I shrugged. "Probably. Look, Marli, I'm just not ready for all that, okay?"

"Okay, okay. I'm gonna pray for you, Carla. I want things to get better for you."

"So do I."

***

Bryan didn't fight me on anything regarding the divorce. He agreed to all of my terms, including us continuing to share custody of the boys. No child support. We'd still exchange custody every other week, and we'd each have the boys for six straight weeks in the summer. Bryan asked for the boys the first six weeks, and I agreed. He would keep the house and pay me half its value since I helped pay the mortgage. I was amazed that he was being so amicable, but then again, I *was* blackmailing him. I wasn't proud of it, but at least it kept him from bothering me, and it made for a smooth divorce process.

When I sat down to tell the boys about the divorce, I was nervous and a little more than apprehensive, but I knew it was something that had to be done. Under different circumstances, I would've liked for Bryan to be with me so that he could answer some of their questions, but I honestly still couldn't stand to be around him, and a part of me still feared him. So I had to take a deep breath, look into my boys' eyes, and give them the news alone.

I was perched on the edge of the coffee table, and the boys were sitting side-by-side on the sofa—both wearing curious expressions. Derek was so much like Bryan now—tall, with golden-brown skin and chocolate eyes. Patrick was a mixture of the two of us, with my darker skin but most of Bryan's features. They were my heart, and my heart ached at having to tell them about the divorce.

"What is it, Mama?" Patrick asked. "Are you sick? You don't have cancer, do you? Amari's mama's got cancer, and she's real sick."

I softened my expression. "No, baby. I'm not sick. It's about me and your daddy."

"Y'all getting back together?" Derek asked, his eyes bright.

My heart sank. "No, baby. We're getting a divorce. This won't change how things are, though. You'll still spend a week with me and a week with him, and you'll spend six whole weeks with each of us in the summer."

Derek frowned. "That's it? I thought y'all was already divorced."

Patrick nodded. "Me, too."

I sat there for a moment, feeling like a fool. What else would they think since we'd been living apart for four years? Here I was, thinking I was making a big announcement, and these boys already had things figured out long before I did.

"Okay, um, do you guys think you need to talk to someone, like a counselor or anything?"

They both frowned, and Derek said, "For what?"

I shrugged. "To talk about your feelings, to help you deal with the divorce. Maybe you're feeling angry or sad about how things are now?"

"Oh, naw, I been over that," Derek said, matter-of-factly.

I frowned and tilted my head to the side. "But you're always so mad. What's that about?"

He shook his head. "Just school and stuff like that. Regular stuff. And I ain't mad all the time, just sometimes."

"Well, it seems like all the time to me," I said.

"Yeah, you do be mad like all the time, dude," Patrick agreed.

"I'm sorry, then. I don't mean to be," Derek said softly.

"Derek, are you sure you're not angry about me and your dad being apart?"

He slightly shrugged his shoulders. "I mean, I wish things were like they used to be. I wish we all lived in the same house. But I guess that ain't gonna happen."

I looked into his eyes. "No, it's not. And I am so sorry, Derek. I'm so sorry. What about you, Patrick?"

He dropped his young eyes. "Yeah, I wish we could all be together, too."

I sighed. "If there was any way I could make that happen for you guys, I would. I promise I would. I love you both so much."

"I love you, too, Mama," Derek said. Patrick nodded in agreement.

I clasped my hands together. "Um, do you guys have any questions for me, about the divorce?"

"You and Daddy gonna marry other people now?" Derek asked.

"Yeah, like my friend, Marshall's, parents? He's got three moms and one dad now," Patrick added.

"You mean, *two* moms?" I asked.

He shook his head. "No, *three*. His dad married another woman and so did his mom, so he has three moms and one dad," Patrick explained.

I looked over at Derek, who just shrugged. I turned back to Patrick. "Um, that's definitely *not* gonna happen. I won't be marrying a woman... or a man, for that matter." I sort of mumbled the last bit. I don't think either of them caught it.

"You gonna have a boyfriend?" Derek asked.

I really regretted asking them if they had any questions. It was hard enough explaining the birds and the bees to Derek a few years earlier. I hadn't even broached that subject with Patrick yet. But discussing the possibility of me or Bryan dating or getting married again was uncomfortable, to say the least.

"I don't think so, Derek. I don't plan to have a boyfriend. I just wanna concentrate on you two guys."

Derek shrugged. "It'd be okay if you did have a boyfriend. I wouldn't care as long as he treated you right."

Patrick nodded his eleven-year-old head like he knew what Derek was talking about.

I stifled a smile and said, "Well, that's good to know. Anything else?"

They sat there with pensive expressions on their faces for a full minute before they said, "No," almost in unison.

I slapped my hands against my jean-clad thighs. "Well, okay then. Um, as soon as school is out, you're gonna spend some time with your dad, and after that, you'll be with me for the rest of the summer."

"Okay," Patrick said.

Derek nodded.

"Okay, well, I'm gonna go to my room for a little bit. Oh, and we might be moving this summer to a better place."

"Okay," they both said.

I hugged them both, thinking to myself that that was a little too easy, but I was thankful that they took things so well. Once in my room, I stretched across the bed and closed my eyes. I was deep in thought when I heard a soft knock at the door. "Mama, can I come in?"

I recognized Derek's voice, sat up in the bed, and said, "Sure, come on in."

He walked in and sat at the foot of the bed. "I didn't want to ask you this in front of Patrick, but is Daddy gay?"

My heart thumped in my chest. I was right in thinking that things had gone too easily, because Derek had been waiting to lower the hammer. I swallowed hard and took a moment to measure my words.

"Why do you ask that?" I said softly, watching his face.

He looked me in the eye. "Because he was with that dude that night."

I dropped my eyes. I'd hoped—I don't know what I'd hoped for. I wished things were different, though. This wasn't a conversation I ever wanted to have with my own child. Derek had never brought that night up before, and neither had I. Maybe I should have. "I don't know, Derek. Only your dad can answer that question."

He nodded, and after a few seconds of silence, asked, "Is that why you guys are not together anymore?"

I reached over and held his warm hand in mine. "Things just didn't work out between us. That's all."

"Are you gonna be better now?"

I frowned slightly, taken aback by his question. "What do you mean, *better*? I'm fine, Derek."

"No you're not. You're sad all the time. You never smile."

"Oh… well, I'm working on being better. Don't you worry about me, okay? As long as you're happy, I'm happy." I forced a smile and hugged him tightly while thinking to myself that my boys were definitely not babies anymore.

8

"Another One"

I woke up to the sound of loud banging. I was so disoriented that at first, I didn't know where it was coming from, but it didn't take me long to pull myself together and notice that the sound was coming from my front door. I stumbled to my feet, wrapped a robe around my body, and shuffled past the packed boxes scattered throughout my apartment to the front door. My first thought was that whoever was at the door was going to wake up the boys. Then I remembered that they were with Bryan for six weeks.

I checked the peephole, and there stood Bryan on the other side of the door. I sighed and shook my head. "Bryan, what are you doing here this time of night? Where are the boys?"

"They're right here. Let us in."

I quickly unlocked the door and opened it. "What's going on?" I asked as Bryan and the boys filed into the apartment.

Neither of them said a word. They just walked into the living room and stood around me, staring at me.

"Derek, Patrick, what's wrong?" I turned to Bryan. "Why are you—"

Before I could finish my statement, Bryan punched me dead in the mouth. I stumbled backward and looked at the boys. They just stood there and stared, with lifeless expressions on their faces.

"Bryan..." I whimpered as I held a hand over my rapidly swelling lips. "Why are you doing this?"

"You know why!" he yelled. Then he punched me in the jaw. I spun around and landed on my knees. I quickly scrambled to my feet and ran from the living room to my bedroom. I tried to shut the door, but Bryan blocked it with his foot. He shoved me backward, and I fell onto the floor, hitting my head on the edge of the dresser on my way down. My head throbbed as Bryan crawled on top of me and, in a harsh whisper, said, "You will always be mine." He ripped my underwear off. "*This* will always be mine." He gripped my head in his hands and lifted my face up to meet his, then he kissed me. He smiled and began to shake me. "Wake up!" he screamed.

My eyes popped open, and I found myself in my own bed, hoarse and drenched in sweat. Derek and Patrick stood over me with concerned looks on their faces.

"Mama, you okay? You were screaming in your sleep," Derek said.

"You had a nightmare?" Patrick asked in a timid voice.

"Yeah," I said as I sat up on the side of the bed and tried to calm my galloping heart. "But I'm okay now. You two go back to bed."

"You sure?" Derek asked.

"Yeah, I'm fine. Go back to bed."

The boys both hugged me before leaving my room and closing the door behind them. I walked into the bathroom, sat on the toilet, and cried.

***

That dream really messed with my head. I didn't eat or sleep for days afterwards, and I felt like I was losing my mind. If I closed my eyes for even a second, just to rest them, the dream would start to replay in my head. I didn't feel safe in my home. I didn't feel safe *anywhere.*

The straw that broke the camel's back was an incident that occurred one afternoon, about a week after I had the dream. I was sitting at a red light, waiting for it to change, when a car pulled up beside me. I glanced over, and when I saw Bryan in the driver's side staring at me, my foot hit the accelerator almost involuntarily. I shot through the intersection, narrowly missing the cars that had the right of way. I floored the pedal, speeding down the street, before finally pulling onto the lot of a gas station. I parked the car at a pump and tried to calm my throbbing heart. I closed my eyes and tried to breathe and tried not to cry. I was so confused and afraid, but at the same time, I didn't even really understand my own actions. What was I running from? He hadn't bothered me in weeks. I hadn't even seen him face-to-face since our last divorce hearing. He dropped the boys off at his mother's house for me to pick them up, and I dropped them off at my mother's house for him to pick them up. He'd been very agreeable and cordial with me. So what was with the dream? Why was I so terrified of him?

I opened my eyes to the sound of someone or something pecking on my window. It was Bryan, and my first instinct was to put the car in gear and tear out of that gas station. He saw my hand move and said, "Wait, don't leave," through the window. "I just wanna talk, Carla."

I took a deep breath and told myself that we were in a public place and that I had no need to be afraid of him. He wasn't stupid enough to assault me in public. I pressed the button and let the window down. "Yes?" I said softly.

"Why'd you take off like that? You could've been hit. Are you okay?"

I stared at him for a minute. There were many words swimming around in my head at that moment, and none of them were, "Yes, I'm okay," or, "I'm cool," or, "I'm peachy keen!" Was he serious? Surely, he was joking. I lowered my head, and the next thing I knew, I was laughing. I was laughing *uncontrollably*—the type of laughter that brings tears to your eyes and makes your stomach cramp.

Bryan frowned and then gave me a mildly confused expression. "Something funny?"

I nodded. "Yeah, *very* funny."

He backed away from the car and shook his head. "You're crazy."

For some reason, that made me laugh harder. I put my car in gear and pulled off of the gas station lot, and I laughed all the way home.

***

"I'm losing it, Marli, and I wouldn't even care if I didn't need to be sane to raise my sons," I said into the phone as I pulled onto the street, leaving my mother's house. I'd left the boys there, all packed up and ready to spend six weeks with their father.

"You're not losing it. You're traumatized. If what happened to you happened to me, that dream you had would've messed me up, too."

"Yeah, but I can't freak out every time I cross paths with Bryan. Pine Bluff is a small town. I'm bound to run into him from time to time."

"Then maybe you should leave for a while. The boys are with him for six weeks, and you're still on leave from your job. Come stay with us. Maybe the change of scenery will do you good."

"I'm sorry, girl, but I can't come back to the scene of the crime. Can't do it."

"You've visited us before. What's so different now?"

"I don't know. *I'm* different. More crap has happened to me."

"Well, you need to do *something*, Carla. You can't keep going without sleep. That's just unhealthy."

I closed my eyes and rubbed my forehead. "You're right, but I can't come to St. Louis. And my brain is so fried, I can't think of anywhere else to go."

She held the phone as we both racked our brains, then she said, "Hey, what about the cabin Chris bought me for my birthday last year? You could stay there, and Bryan would have no idea where you were. He wouldn't need to know, either. As long as he could reach you by phone, you could keep in touch with the boys."

I thought for a moment. "That's actually a very good idea, but I'm supposed to be moving, remember? But to tell the truth, I haven't even been looking."

"Are you under a lease?"

"No."

"Then go ahead and pay your rent for that place, lock it up, and go to the cabin for a few weeks. Maybe when you get back home, your mind will be clear enough to find another place."

I leaned against the back of my couch and felt all of the tension in my head begin to dissipate. It was a good idea, a *great* idea, actually. And as I sat there and pondered it, I knew it was just what I needed. "Okay, I think I'll do that," I said.

"Oh, I'm so glad!" Marli said, sounding relieved. "One of the neighbors, Mrs. Cook, has the spare key. I'll call and let her know you're coming. You're gonna love it!"

I really, really hoped she was right.

9

"On My Own"

Chris's and Marli's cabin was located in Garland County, Arkansas, a few miles outside of Hot Springs, on Cook Road. I drove for miles on a bumpy paved road before it became a bumpy dirt road lined with overgrown trees and high grass. My only thought was that it must've been a mess trying to drive that road in the rain. Following Marli's directions, I drove another mile before turning left onto yet another dirt road. A half a mile later, I pulled into the driveway of Mrs. Elda Cook, the neighbor who was in possession of the key to my temporary home, and also, according to Marli, the woman from whom Chris had bought the cabin. As a matter of fact, Elda Cook's family owned most of the land in that area, hence the name of the road. At one point, this had all been family property, from the small lake that sat in the center of the plot of land to the cabins that surrounded it.

I took a deep breath, climbed out of my SUV, and made my way up to the front door of her rustic-looking home. I stepped onto the chair-lined porch and knocked on the door. I glanced at my surroundings. Trees, trees, and more trees. I was truly out in the middle of nowhere. I definitely had no reason to fear Bryan way out there. There was no way he'd be able to locate me.

The heavy wooden door slowly opened, and a small, frail-looking white lady appeared behind the screen door. "Ms. Tooley?" she asked with raised eyebrows.

It took me a second to remember that I'd taken my maiden name back after the divorce was final, so I stood there with a blank look on my face before finally saying, "Yes. Mrs. Cook?"

She nodded and gave me a smile. "Yes, well, come on in. Let me get the key for you."

I followed her into the house, and the heavenly aroma of coffee instantly filled my nose. I stood just inside the door as she walked further into the house, stopped, and turned around. "Well, come on. Don't be shy," she said.

I wasn't used to complete strangers inviting me into their homes so warmly. Yes, all of Arkansas is in the south, but in Pine Bluff, the new era had hardened a lot of people. Crime had placed cautiousness before hospitality. So I was still hesitant as I walked into her living room and took a seat on the sofa she gestured to. To my surprise, she sat across from me in a recliner. The only thing on my mind was getting that key and getting settled into the cabin. Mrs. Cook, it seemed, had other plans.

"Well, Marli tells me that you and she have been friends since you were girls," she said as she crossed her thin legs at the ankle and settled back in her chair.

"Yes, ma'am. Marli is my oldest and dearest friend."

She nodded and picked up an oversized mug. She took a sip from it and shook her head. "Oh, goodness! Where are my manners? Would you like some coffee, dear? It's a special blend my daughter sent me from Brazil. She and her husband are world travelers of sorts."

"Oh, really? Well, yes, ma'am. I'd love some. It smells delicious." I was ready to get to my cabin, but good coffee was a weakness of mine, and there was no way I was turning down some authentic, *Brazilian* coffee.

"Okay, be right back."

I watched as she stood from the chair and slowly made her way to the kitchen. As I waited for her to return, I glanced around the room at the paintings of deer, trees, and fish that graced the walls. There were also family portraits galore. There was an entire wall dedicated to pictures of children and adults alike. If those were her family members, she was surely blessed with a large clan.

She returned with another oversized mug in one hand and a few packets of sugar and creamer in the other. She handed everything to me and said, "I forgot to ask how you take it, so I decided to let you fix it up yourself. Oh, shoot! Let me get you a spoon."

I shook my head and held up a hand to stop her. "Don't worry about that. I take my coffee black."

"Really?" she said as she shuffled around the coffee table back to her chair. "Then you're a true coffee drinker, like me."

I smiled as I brought the mug to my lips and took a small sip. I had never, in all my days, tasted anything so full of flavor! I had downed nearly half of the cup before I came up for air. "This is so good!" I exclaimed.

Mrs. Cook nodded with a smile. "Isn't it? I do hope my daughter sends me some more. I'll soon run out of it."

"Well, thank you for sharing it with me."

"Not a problem, dear. I hope you'll find whatever you're looking for in that cabin."

I frowned as I sat the cup on the table. What had Marli told her about me? "What makes you think I'm looking for anything?" I asked.

She clasped her hands in her lap and sighed. "Honey, nobody

decides to come way out here, to the middle of nowhere, alone, unless they're looking for something—peace, inspiration. You don't have to tell me what it is; I just hope you find it here."

I dropped my eyes slightly. "Well, thank you."

She reached into a bowl sitting on the end table next to her chair and unearthed a key chain. She dangled it in her hand. "I know you've been waiting on this. Probably wondering why the old woman is holding you captive." She chuckled, and I smiled, because yes, that was exactly what I was wondering.

"I get lonesome sometimes, you know? All of my family is either dead and gone, or just gone. I'm the only Cook left on this land. No one seems to care about the old homestead now. So I've been selling these cabins one-by-one, and the ones that haven't been sold, I've been renting out. At least that way, I have some neighbors. There's Marli and Chris, who bought the one just up the road—I sure do love them, such a sweet pair those two."

I smiled. "Yes, ma'am. They are."

"There're six cabins in all, including mine. There's one right next to yours. There's a nice fella, a professor, renting that one. Then, across the lake are three more—all rented out to families for the summer."

I nodded. "I see. Kinda crowded around here then, huh?"

She shook her head. "Not really. That lake is bigger than you think. You might never cross paths with the folks across the lake, but you're close to the fella next door. I remember when these cabins were full of Cooks and Wainwrights. The Wainwrights were my folk. My husband and I bought this land so the family could all be together." She sighed and shook her head. "Well, anyhow, here's your key." She reached across the coffee table and handed it to me.

"Thank you," I said as I clutched the key and stood from the sofa.

She stood and led me to the front door. "Don't be shy. Feel free to drop in and visit with me whenever you like. Oh, wait here for just a sec."

She scurried off, and I stood at the screen door and watched as an old pick-up truck slowly approached. The driver honked his horn as he passed by.

"That's your neighbor," Mrs. Cook said, startling me. I turned around to find her holding a paper sack out to me. "Here you go. Some coffee for the road."

I took the sack from her and peered inside at the colorful coffee bag. "Oh, no, Mrs. Cook. I can't take the last of your coffee." I tried to hand it back to her, but she wouldn't take it.

"I insist. I'm sure my daughter will send me some more. Think of it as a 'welcome to the lake' gift. I hope you enjoy your stay, dear."

I smiled. "Me, too. Thank you so much."

***

Marli's cabin was an exact replica of Mrs. Cook's from the outside, as was the neighboring cabin, which couldn't have been more than fifty feet away. Both cabins faced the road. The backs of the cabins included steps that led from the back decks out onto a short pier over the lake. It was beautiful and peaceful, and I felt safe for the first time in a long time.

I looked over at the other cabin as I lifted the back gate of my SUV and dragged my suitcase out onto the ground. I thought to myself that it would probably be a good idea to introduce myself to my neighbor, but I was already tired from a combination of the long drive and the many nights of missed sleep I'd experienced. It was going to be all I could do to make it up the steps and into the cabin. I hoped I had the strength to make it all the way into the bedroom before collapsing.

When I finally made it inside, I dropped my bags by the door and whispered, "Home, sweet home."

10

"Excuse Me"

I reached across the bed and grabbed my cell phone. "Hello?" I mumbled.

"Hey!! You all settled in?" Marli chirped into the phone.

"Kind of. I was so tired when I got here, I went straight to bed. My bags are still sitting by the door." I opened my eyes and realized that it was dark outside. "Dang! I've been asleep all day!"

"Well, you haven't slept well in a while. You needed to catch up. So what do you think of the place?"

"It's nice, Marli. Really peaceful. And Mrs. Cook is a sweetheart. I haven't met my neighbor yet, though. I hope he's nice, too."

"He?"

"Don't even go there. I'm over men, remember? And besides, Mrs. Cook said he's a college professor, and judging from the ancient truck parked in front of his cabin, he's probably a seventy-year-old man with thick glasses and bad teeth or something."

She chuckled. "Why he gotta be all of that?"

"I *hope* he is. I don't need for him to be fine."

She laughed again. "Well, I'll let you go back to sleep. Be checking the mail, I sent you something."

"Okay... thanks, again, and thank Chris for me. I really appreciate you guys for letting me stay here."

"You know it's no problem. Talk to you later."

"Okay."

I laid my phone on the bed, closed my eyes, and thirty minutes later, found myself still awake, and on top of that, hungry. I wasn't about to try to navigate the dirt road in the dark since I knew there were no streetlights. So I wasn't going to be able to go to the store until the morning. I lay there for five or ten more minutes before deciding to head out to my vehicle to get the snacks I'd bought before I left Pine Bluff. I was too tired to bring them in when I first arrived. Maybe they would tide me over until I could buy some groceries in the morning.

I was still fully dressed, so I just slipped on my shoes and headed outside. It was so quiet that it actually felt kind of strange. There was a slight breeze, which made the night air feel pleasant, inviting. I decided I'd take my snacks out on the back deck and enjoy them and the weather. Once out on the deck, I opened my bag of chips and munched on them as I stared out at the lake. *Yes, this is just what I needed.*

I was sitting in the darkness, enjoying my chips and warm soda, when I heard a door creak open. I turned my head to see my neighbor's back door slowly opening, casting light into what had been almost total darkness, save the reflection of the moon on the lake. I watched, waiting for a glimpse of the professor. A second later, a form stepped out of the cabin and quickly shut the door, eliminating the light and forcing me to strain my eyes to see him. He stood in the shadows of the deck for a while, and I started to wonder if he knew I was watching, so I turned toward the water. A minute later, I saw him walking down the pier. The moonlight seemed to follow him. My eyes were glued to him as he stopped at the edge of the pier and shed his clothes. I got an eyeful of his body—his tall, lean, beautiful, naked body. Whoever he was, he was gorgeous! He had the broadest shoulders I'd ever seen, and there was not an inch of fat on his body. Nothing but well-defined muscle. He wasn't bulky, but powerful-looking nonetheless. I leaned forward as he faced the lake, spread his arms wide, and lifted his head to the sky. Then he leaned forward until he fell into the water. I don't know why, but I stood and walked to the edge of the deck, my eyes searching for the stranger, waiting for him to emerge from the water. After a few agonizing seconds, his head popped up, and he shook it back and forth and squeezed the water from his shoulder-length hair before dipping back beneath the water's surface. *Who is he?* I wondered. From what I could see, he looked too young to be a professor. Was he the professor's son? His lover*? Oh, please be his lover, because you are too fine to be straight and living this close to me,* I thought.

I reclaimed my seat and watched him like he was an episode of the TV show, *Scandal*—with my bottom on the edge of the seat and my mouth hung open. He continued to swim and dip, and thirty minutes later, he climbed back onto the pier, retrieved his clothes, and disappeared back into his cabin. After I calmed my throbbing heart, I went inside of my own cabin and climbed back into bed.

***

When I awakened the next morning, I fixed myself a cup of Mrs. Cook's Brazilian coffee and decided to tour the cabin, since I'd been too tired to do it when I first arrived. It had the same layout as Mrs.

Cook's place. There was an open floor plan—no walls separated the living room from the kitchen and dining areas. It was very clean, and Marli and Chris had decorated it with modern, rustic furniture. Gorgeous family photos hung on the walls. I smiled at the faces of my friend and her beautiful family, and then my eyes clouded a little as I thought about my own broken family and my poor sons, who would spend the rest of their childhoods being shuffled between me and Bryan.

I shook my head and told myself not to go there. I'd let Bryan hurt me too many times already. I was in the middle of nowhere, looking for peace of mind, and up until the moment I conjured him up in my thoughts, I'd found it. He was not going to take away the tiny bit of sanity I had regained in the few hours I'd been in Garland County. So I squared my shoulders and continued my tour.

There were two bedrooms and one bathroom. I had already claimed the master bedroom for myself and would finish unpacking my bags when I returned from the grocery store. That was a trip that couldn't wait, since the beautiful, stainless steel refrigerator was completely empty.

I made the bed before taking a quick shower and heading out. I noticed that the professor's truck was already gone as I climbed into my vehicle. I wondered if his skinny-dipping guest was home. *I wouldn't mind seeing that body in the daylight,* I thought. Then I shook my head. *No, you don't,* I scolded myself. *You are done with men. Done!* I sighed as I cranked up my car and pulled off of the gravel driveway onto the dirt road.

In no time, I was walking the aisles of the supermarket, picking up the essentials—coffee, tea, milk, eggs, bread, etc. And a few non-essentials—candy, chips, cookies. I could afford the goodies. Over the past two or three months, I'd lost nearly forty pounds and had had to buy all new clothes. I hated the way I looked. I hadn't been that thin since high school, and my head was too big for my body. I seriously looked like a human bobble head. Hopefully, I'd be able to put on a little weight over the next few weeks.

After I finished my grocery shopping, I dropped by the dollar store and picked up some paper plates, plastic cups, and silverware. I was *not* washing dishes during my vacation. I picked up toilet tissue, paper towels, and feminine products, too, since "Aunt Flo" would be making a visit soon.

Before I knew it, I was crawling along the dirt road again, headed back to my temporary home. I waved at Mrs. Cook, who was sitting on her porch when I passed her house. By the time I made it to my cabin, I was nearly starving, *and* I had to pee. I unlatched the back gate of my truck, grabbed one of the bags, and rushed inside the cabin to use the bathroom. When I walked back out the door, I noticed that the rest of my bags were sitting on my front porch, and the truck's back gate was closed. I glanced at my neighbor's house and noticed that the old truck was parked in front.

I quickly took the bags inside and rushed back outside. My intention was to thank my neighbor, since I was sure he'd brought my bags to the porch, but the truck was gone again. He'd left just that quickly.

I went on about the business of unpacking groceries and clothing, trying to make my temporary home feel homey. I did so with a constant curiosity about my neighbor. When I unpacked a small picture of the boys, I smiled and decided to call Derek's cell phone. He answered on the first ring.

"Hey, Mama."

"Hey, D. How're you guys doing?" I responded.

"We're cool. You okay?"

"I'm fine, but I miss you guys. Where's your brother?"

"Right here. Hold on."

"Hey, Carla." I tightly shut my eyes as Bryan's voice invaded my ear—*not* Patrick's. And even though we were miles apart and he had no idea where I was, my heart still sped up, and my hand began to shake.

"Bryan, uh… I was holding for Patrick."

"He's right here. How've you been?"

"Fine."

"That's good. The boys say you're at Marli's?"

"Yeah." Well, it wasn't a complete lie. Technically, I *was* at Marli's.

"That's nice. Well, here's Patrick. Good hearing your voice."

I didn't respond. There was no sense in me pretending it was good to hear *his voice*.

I chatted with Patrick for a few minutes before hanging up and starting on my dinner. I decided I'd call and check with my parents in the morning. They were the only people besides Marli, Chris, and Mrs. Cook who knew exactly where I was.

***

I was sleeping peacefully when I woke up out of the blue around 11:00 P.M. I lay there listening to the quiet for a little while before deciding to get up and check the house. There was that thought that often sat at the back of my mind since I separated from Bryan—did I lock the doors?

I walked through the house in my short pajama set and bare feet and checked the front door. Then I headed to the kitchen to check the back door. Both were locked. As I passed the window over the kitchen sink, I caught a glimpse of something that stopped me in my tracks. There he was again—standing at the end of the pier, arms spread, head held toward the sky, body completely naked. I stared at him and watched as he leaned forward until he landed in the water.

I stood at the window and watched him—my mind full of questions. There was something about him, whoever he was, that seemed to draw me in. I couldn't look away, and I couldn't move. He commanded my attention, and my heart rate increased with each stroke he made in the water. Whoever he was, whatever he was to the professor, he intrigued me. So much so that when I finally left my post at the window and climbed back into bed that night, my dreams were of him.

11

"Trippin'"

The next morning, I called home for an update from my parents, and other than Grandma Tooley having a slight cold, things were fine with them.

"I'm glad y'all are doing okay," I said as I sat on my front porch, my eyes glued to my neighbor's truck. I was hoping to see the mystery man in the daylight.

"Having better dreams now, huh?" Mama asked.

I took the phone from my ear and looked at it. Then I put it back up to my ear. "What?"

"You heard me. I said, you're having better dreams."

"Yeah, I guess so."

"You guess so? Well, I'm glad for you. You sound better. I bet you look better, too. I was worried that what Bryan did to you was going to completely destroy you. Glad to see it didn't."

I held the phone. I hadn't told my mother the whole truth of what happened with Bryan, not about the rape or even that he'd been with a man. I'd only told her that he cheated, but I knew she knew it all, just as she always did.

"I'll let you go. I hope you'll soon make your reality as good as your dreams." And with that, she hung up.

I sat there and closed my eyes and wondered why she thought I had the power to make anything a reality—especially all of the things that happened in that dream. That dream was all about touching and loving and a passion that made me wet my sheets with sweat. How could that become a reality when all I knew of the man in the dreams was that he had a beautiful body and lived next door with the old professor? How in the world—

"Good morning." The voice was friendly and masculine. When I opened my eyes, I saw him standing at the foot of my front porch steps—shoulder-length hair blowing in the wind, eyes hidden behind sunglasses. But that *body*. Though it was covered in worn, blue jeans and a faded, yellow t-shirt, I'd know it anywhere…

This was the mysterious skinny-dipper, *literally* the man of my dreams.

I couldn't speak, so I just sat there with my mouth hung open. Sweat poured down my back though it was barely seventy degrees that morning. He removed his eyewear, revealing chocolate eyes that drew me in so deeply, I was afraid I'd get lost in them. He stepped up onto the porch. Looking down at me, he extended a hand and smiled. "I've been meaning to come over and introduce myself. I'm Michael Ross, your neighbor."

Slowly, I felt my senses return as I gripped the hand of the man I'd basically been stalking the past couple of days. He held my hand firmly as he shook it, and that brief touch of his bronze skin awakened all of my female senses. It was as if the man oozed some potent form of testosterone, because he made me think of nothing but being a woman, *his* woman.

"Uh-um-uh, I'm… Carla Tooley. Nice to meet you."

He nodded.

"Oh, and th… thanks for helping me with my groceries

yesterday."

"You're welcome. Well, I promise to be a good neighbor. No loud parties or anything like that. I'm preparing to teach a new class in the fall, so I'll be quietly reading."

My eyes widened. "*You're* the professor? But you're too young!"

He shook his head. "Mrs. Cook likes to call me that, but I'm just a history instructor at UALR. I'm working on my doctorate, but I'm not a professor... and I'm forty."

Forty sure looks good on you, I thought. "Oh... well, nice to meet you." *Goodness! This man is so fine, I'm repeating myself!*

"Same here... let me know if you need anything."

This time, when he extended his hand, I noticed a wedding band on his other hand. My heart calmed a bit as I shook his hand and watched him walk away.

***

"You planned this, Marli. I *know* you did!" I shouted into the phone.

"Carla, have you completely lost it? How can I plan who Mrs. Cook rents her property to?"

"I don't know. Shoot, you probably own that cabin, too. And you probably recruited his fine tail to move in. I can't *believe* this!"

"Carla, do you hear what you're saying? Come on, now. You need to get ahold of yourself."

"I have sworn to myself that I am done with men, and I mean it. But the finest man on Earth is living next to me, and he keeps skinny dipping all over the freakin' place. How am I supposed to deal with this?"

"Um, *I'm* married to the finest man on the planet."

"Okay, the finest non-white man. I think he's Mexican or something." I shook my head at the thought of him. "My only consolation is that he was wearing a wedding ring. That's the only thing that is keeping me from running over there and throwing myself at him, because, guess what? The prayers didn't work. My vagina is *not* numb."

She laughed.

"What are you laughing at?"

"You! You called me screaming in the phone like the cabin was on fire. It's just a *man*, and from what you've told me, a nice, handsome man."

"But I'm over—"

"Yeah, yeah, I know! And I don't date white men. Remember that?"

"That's different. You were just scared of being hurt."

"So are you, Carla," she said softly.

I held the phone for a moment, my voice caught in my throat.

"I'm sorry if you didn't want to hear that, but it's the truth."

"No, it's not. I'm just... I don't want to make the same mistakes again," I said.

"What mistakes? Trusting Bryan, falling in love with him, and marrying him?"

"That, and going on a bender like I did in St. Louis and almost abandoning my kids. It's not being hurt that I'm afraid of. It's my reaction to being hurt."

"Yeah, I guess I know what you mean. Um... did you get the package I sent?"

I shook my head. "No, I haven't checked the mailbox since I've been here."

"Well, check it today. It should've arrived by now."

"Okay."

"Okay. I love you, girl. I'm always praying for you."

"I know, and I appreciate it. Love you, too." I hung up and decided to take a nap. I'd check the mail later. That conversation and the feelings it dredged up had drained me.

12
"Pray Me Well"

I ended up sleeping right through dinnertime. As a matter of fact, I slept until around two o'clock the next morning. What awakened me was a menstrual cramp sent straight from the bowels—or uterus—of hell, so I climbed out of bed and went into the bathroom to put on a pad to catch the expected flow. To my surprise, my panties were soaked with blood. I changed my underwear, put on a pad, and took a pain reliever before climbing back into bed to find a blood stain on the fitted sheet. I groaned. The pain reliever hadn't kicked in yet, and the cramps were kicking my butt. I would've rather slept on the floor than change the sheets at that moment. I decided to put a towel over the spot and got back into bed.

I woke up an hour later to what had to be the worst pain I'd felt in my life and a completely saturated maxi pad. My period tended to be heavier when I was under stress but never *that* heavy. At the rate things were going, I was going to need a blood transfusion soon. I crawled out of bed and walked back to the toilet where I sat for a full ten minutes before I gathered up the strength to stand up. When I turned to flush the toilet I saw that it was full of blood and blood clots. *What is going on?* I wondered.

I was up and down for the rest of the morning—close to overdosing on the pain reliever.

Around 8:00 A.M., I was in the kitchen fixing a cup of tea, in the hopes that it would help sooth my aching pelvic region, when I heard a knock at the front door. "Coming!" I yelled as I slowly made my way from the kitchen to the living room. I unlocked and opened the door to find a smiling Michael Ross standing on my porch.

"Good morning," he said. "I was wondering if you'd like to have breakfast with me."

I opened my mouth to respond, but before I could, I collapsed into his arms.

***

"A miscarriage?" I said, repeating the emergency room doctor's words. "How could I have a miscarriage when I wasn't even pregnant?"

"I assure you that you *were* pregnant, Ms. Tooley," the petite doctor said.

I shook my head. My face was fixed in a permanent frown. "But I haven't missed a period. I didn't *feel* pregnant."

She gave me a thoughtful look. "Well, some women just don't experience any pregnancy symptoms. It's actually not that uncommon."

I rested my hand on my stomach. "What happened? Why... why did I lose it?"

"I can't pinpoint it without running some tests. Would you like for me to do that?"

I shook my head. "No."

"Are you sure?"

I swiped at the single tear that rolled down my cheek and nodded my head.

"Do you want me to tell your husband, or do you want to tell him? He can come back now."

My frown deepened. "Husband?"

"The gentleman who came in with you." She glance down at the papers she held in her hand. "Michael?"

My face relaxed, but only a little. "Um… sure. You can send him back here."

A few minutes later, I found myself face-to-face with the benevolent Mr. Michael Ross. His eyes were full of concern as he slowly walked into the room and softly shut the door behind him. He rolled the sleeves of his plaid shirt up toward his elbow and slightly nodded his head. "Hey, you okay?"

"Yeah, I'm okay. Did you bring me here?"

He moved a little closer to the bed, stopped, and shoved his hands into the back pockets of his jeans. "Yeah... I didn't know what else to do."

"Thank you. And you waited? You didn't have to do that."

He shrugged. "I wanted to be sure you were okay. What happened? There was blood——a lot of blood."

"Did it mess up the inside of your truck? I'm so sorr——"

He held up a hand. "It's okay. Don't worry about my truck. What… what happened?"

I closed my eyes and sighed. "I..."

"I'm sorry. You don't have to tell me. It's none of my business.

I'll just wait out in the lobby for you."

"No, I've been enough trouble. I'll just... I'll get a ride."

"With who? Taxis don't go out that far. Don't worry. It's no trouble."

"Well, thanks. I should be able to go home soon."

"Okay. I'll be waiting."

He grasped the door handle, released it, and turned to face me again. "I'm glad you're okay."

I gave him a weak smile. "Thank you. Me, too."

A nurse burst into the room, nearly hitting Michael with the door. He wore a bewildered look on his face as the nurse, who hadn't noticed him, rushed to my bedside.

"Have you ever had a miscarriage before, Ms. Tooley?" she asked.

Michael's eyes widened as he slipped out the door.

I sighed softly. "No, I haven't," I answered.

She handed me some paperwork—discharge instructions. She told me to take it easy for a couple of days and to wait a couple of months before trying to get pregnant again. I just nodded. I didn't see the use in telling this woman, who I'd probably never see again, that I wasn't trying to get pregnant in the first place, or that, since I always made sure Bryan used protection, it had to be the rape that resulted in this pregnancy. I didn't tell her any of that. I just nodded, and when it was time to leave, I let Michael wheel me out to his truck and help me inside. Once he pulled off of the hospital parking lot and began making his way from the town of Hot Springs back to our lakeside utopia, I remembered the prescription for an antibiotic the nurse had handed me.

"Uh... can we stop by a drug store?" I asked. "I forgot about this prescription I need to fill."

He glanced at me. "Sure."

We stopped at a Walgreens, and he helped me out of his truck. I was a little groggy from the pain medication and was thankful that he held my arm and escorted me inside. We had to wait thirty minutes, but Michael never left my side. Once we were back in his truck, on our way to Cook Lake, I said, "Thank you, again... for everything. I don't know what I would've done without your help. I mean, you even drove back to my cabin and brought me my purse and some clothes to wear home. *Thank you*."

He smiled at me. "Just being neighborly."

I shook my head. "This is way past neighborly. You don't know me. It takes a special kindness to help a stranger like you've helped me. I'm gonna have to figure out a way to repay you."

"No repayment necessary. And I *do* know you. I know your spirit. You're a good person. I can sense it."

I dropped my eyes and then glanced up at him again. He was so handsome, *too* handsome, really. Good thing he was married. "Thank you. I sense the same in you. Your wife is a very blessed woman."

His smile faded. Almost instantly, his eyes shifted to the ring on his hand, and he dropped his hand from the steering wheel to the side of his body. "I'm a widower," he said softly.

I felt a crazy mixture of sorrow and relief. "Oh, I'm so sorry."

"She was very sick. She was sick when I married her, so I always knew that our time together would be short. It's been three years, and I still can't bring myself to take this ring off."

I nodded. "You still miss her. That's understandable. It's not easy losing someone you love." I felt my own heart begin to ache. Bryan was still alive, but our love was definitely dead, and I missed our love.

"Do you... do you wanna talk about what happened to you this morning?" he asked.

I shook my head. "Not really."

"Okay." He sounded a little hurt, and I felt bad about my short answer. After all, he'd just shared a part of his life with me.

I rested my head on the back of the seat and glanced over at him. "It wasn't planned. I didn't even know I was pregnant, and the father and I are no longer together, so what happened is for the best. I'm okay with it. There's nothing to talk about."

"Oh, I see. Well, if you change your mind and decide there *is* something to talk about, I'm willing to listen. We might not know each other well, but I've found that new friends can be great friends."

I nodded. "Thanks. I'll keep that in mind."

"Good."

When we finally made it back to my cabin, Michael parked right in front and offered to carry me inside. At that point, the only thought in my mind was, *Why, Jesus? Why is this beautiful man being so nice to me? And why, after what I just went through, am I feeling so attracted to him?*

I told him I could walk. I'd lost a lot of blood, and the medicine still had me a little loopy, but I could stumble my way up the steps and into the cabin. He still helped me, though. Once I was inside and sitting on the couch, he stood in front of me and looked around. "Um... you hungry?" he asked.

"I can fix something. Thanks for everything."

"You sure? I can whip something up for you. I'm a pretty decent cook."

I shook my head. "No... really, I'll be fine."

"Um, okay. If you need anything, I'll be right next door. I'll come back and check on you later."

"Thanks."

After he left, I shuffled to the door and locked it behind him. Then I grabbed a chair from the kitchen table, sat in front of the refrigerator, and made myself a sandwich. I kind of wished I'd let him cook, but he really had done enough. After my cold meal, I climbed into the bed in the second bedroom and slept the rest of the day away.

***

I woke up in the middle of the night, thanks to a full bladder, and decided to take a shower. After showering, I went into the kitchen for a glass of water. While standing at the sink, I saw him through the window. He was at the end of the pier again, naked again, *beautiful* again. He stood there with his arms outstretched and his head back, just like the other nights. But this time, instead of falling into the water, he turned his back to the water, giving me a full frontal view in the uncharacteristically bright moonlight. My mouth dropped open, and I leaned over the sink and brought my face so close to the window that my breath fogged up a small portion of the pane. He fell to his knees and clasped his hands in front of him. He was praying. For some reason, seeing him in that position brought tears to my eyes, and a voice in my head said, *"You should pray, too."* I hadn't prayed in a long time—at least not a real, sincere prayer. So I slowly lowered myself onto my knees and closed my eyes.

For the first time since my ex-husband violated me, for the first time since my divorce, for the first time since losing a baby I had no idea I was carrying, I opened my heart to God. I poured out my soul to Him. I asked Him to help me, to save me from the misery and heaviness that had become my constant companions. I'm not sure how long I was on that kitchen floor, but when I finally stood and peered out the window again, Michael Ross was gone.

13

"Coffee"

The next day, I felt a little better and a little stronger. I knew I needed to talk to someone, maybe Marli, but I just didn't feel like it. When I heard the knock at the door, I really didn't want to answer it, either. So I didn't. I just sat there on the sofa and stared at the door. I knew it had to be Michael. I liked him, maybe too much. I decided to distance myself from him, because I was pretty sure that he liked me, too. And as attracted as I was to him, it wasn't lost on me that, although he was widowed, he was still wearing his ring—a sure sign that he was not totally over his late wife. The only thing worse than me in a relationship with a man would be me in a relationship with a man who's hung up on another woman—dead or alive. That was a whole 'nother load of troubles that I just wasn't mentally prepared to deal with.

I sat in the living room with nothing but my thoughts for most of the day before finally deciding to get a little fresh air. I slowly opened the front door, peeked out to be sure that Michael was nowhere in sight, and crept out onto the porch in my bare feet. I'd only made one step when I felt something under my foot. I looked down to see a small bunch of purple flowers lying on the wooden-planked porch. I slowly stooped to pick them up and held them to my nose. "Lavender," I whispered.

My eyes instantly drifted to Michael's cabin, as I was sure he'd left the flowers. I smiled faintly as I took a seat in the chair and stared out at the dirt road and the trees that lined it. I closed my eyes and soaked in the peace and quiet, and I tried to empty my mind of any bad thoughts. I tried to chase away the hurt and pain that my miscarriage had intensified. I tried to remember the serenity I'd felt after my prayer the night before. And then I whispered another prayer for God to heal my heart.

When I opened my eyes, they rested on the mailbox that sat at the edge of the gravel driveway. I slowly stood and decided that I was strong enough to walk the short distance to check the mail, but as I turned to go back into the house to get a pair of shoes, my knees buckled a bit, and I had to grab the outside wall of the cabin to keep from falling.

"Hey! You okay?!" yelled a voice that came from behind me, followed by rapid footfalls.

I turned my head enough to see Michael Ross trotting toward me. "Yeah, I'm fine. I just wanted some air." I glanced at the flowers I'd left sitting on the chair. "Thank you for the flowers. They're from you, right?"

"Yeah, they are. You're welcome. Come on, let me help you inside," he said as he wrapped his arm around my waist.

My heart thudded. He was so close to me that I could smell his minty breath. His scent—a mixture of cedar and manliness—filled my nose. I could've drowned in his scent. "I-I was gonna check the mail," I stammered.

"I'll check it for you. Come on, let me help you."

I nodded and leaned against him as he helped me back inside and onto the sofa.

"Be right back with your mail," he said as he walked toward the front door.

"And my flowers," I called after him.

A few minutes later, he returned with a small package, the flowers, and a Tupperware bowl in hand. He handed me the package and laid the flowers on the coffee table. Then he lifted the bowl. "Dinner. Want me to warm it up for you?"

I gave him a weak smile. "Sure. What is it?"

He shrugged. "Just some squash casserole I picked up at a restaurant earlier."

"Okay, but you have to eat with me," I said. *Why in the world did I say that?*

He grinned. "Deal."

We shared dinner in my living room. Michael sat across from me in the easy chair, and at first, we ate in silence. Then his voice broke into the quietness. "You gonna open your package?" he asked.

I glanced at the bubble envelope sitting on the end table next to me. "I will later."

He nodded. "You been okay today?"

I looked up at him. "I've been fine, just… just tired."

"I'm sorry for not giving you my cell number. I'll be sure to give it to you before I leave this evening. That way you can call if you need anything."

I laid my bowl and fork down and leaned forward. "You really, *really* have done enough. I don't want to be a burden to you. You didn't come out here to take care of an invalid stranger."

"Why are you so uncomfortable with me helping you?" he asked.

I frowned slightly, taken aback by his statement. "It's not that. It's just that… you don't even know me." Then, for some unknown reason, I began to cry. I totally broke down and sobbed right there in front of him.

He jumped up, rushed over to me, and pulled me into his warm, inviting, manly arms. He felt and smelled like just what I needed and had dreamed of. At that moment, Michael Ross felt like Heaven on Earth.

"I prayed for you last night," he whispered.

I leaned into his chest. "Why?"

"Because you needed me to."

I closed my eyes and tried to stop crying, but I just couldn't.

"Whatever it is, it'll get better," he said into my ear.

I shook my head and pounded my fist against his chest. "No, it won't. No, it won't!"

"Yes, it will. You just have to believe that it will, and you have to give it—all of it—to God."

I buried my face in his chest and cried until I ran out of tears.

***

I woke up on my sofa the next morning to the smell of coffee brewing. Sitting across from me was Michael Ross, who'd evidently kept vigil in my living room all night. He gave me a smile and a slight nod of his head as I lifted myself up on the sofa and stretched. The first thought in my head was that I'd missed out on watching him skinny dip the night before.

"Good morning," he said. "Want some coffee?"

I tried to smile back, but my mouth just wouldn't cooperate. I was embarrassed about my meltdown, and I truly didn't understand this man. I didn't get why he was being so nice to me. I'd never met a man like him, and to top it off, I was growing more attracted to him by the second. "Um… yes, but I can pour myself a cup. You should probably head back to your cabin."

He stood from the chair, and without a word, left the living room. A few seconds later, he returned with a mug of coffee and handed it to me. "Do you know how to cook fish?" he asked as he reclaimed his seat.

I stared down at the mug and tried to figure out if he had suddenly gone deaf. "What?" I said.

He leaned forward, resting his elbows on his knees. "Fish. Can you cook fish? I was thinking about going fishing today—at the lake. If I catch any, would you be able to cook them? If not, I can. Or maybe we could cook them together?"

I sighed as I sat up straight and looked at him. "You can leave now."

He stood from the chair and walked back into the kitchen. I waited to hear the back door open and close, but instead, he walked back into the living room with another mug of coffee, sat down in the chair, and took a sip. "This really is some good coffee," he said. "This is my second cup. I hope you don't mind."

I leaned forward with a frown on my face. "Is there something wrong with you? Do I need to say it in Spanish or something? I said, *you can leave now.* Please leave. Go home! ¡Vámonos!"

It was his turn to frown. "I'm not too good with Spanish, but I'm pretty sure that *vámonos* doesn't mean 'go home.'"

"Okay, wrong language. What are you, anyway? Italian, Asian? Is it acceptable in your culture to stay somewhere even when you're not welcome?"

He chuckled lightly. "Wow… okay, first of all, I'm Cherokee, and my culture is the culture of North Carolinians, because that is where I'm from. Now, I'm not leaving you, because you need me here. You're sick and weak, and something is bothering you, because you spent the night tossing and turning and yelling in your sleep. I'm going to help you, because there's no one else around to do it. If there was, you would've called them by now."

"I don't get you! *You do not know me.* I'm a stranger to you. Why are you doing this?!"

"Because I feel compelled to do it."

I shook my head. "No, you want something from me. Well, I'ma tell you right now, you ain't gonna get it! You ain't getting nothing here!"

He tilted his head to the side and lifted one eyebrow. "What is it that you think I want?"

I stood to my feet. "You know what I'm talking about." I turned to leave the room and nearly fell. Michael hurried to me and caught me before I hit the floor.

"When I was praying, I asked God to help you. He told me that *I* was supposed to do it. That's all I'm trying to do. I don't want anything from you."

I looked up at him for a moment and nodded. There was no sense in denying the fact that I needed someone there with me. And if he was on a mission from God, I knew I was definitely fighting a losing battle, but still...

"Um, can you let go of me?" I asked softly.

He obliged and even backed away a little.

"Look," I said. "I appreciate you for all of your help, but I just… I need to be alone. I'm trying to work through some things, and I need to do it alone. Understand?" I looked up at him, my eyes pleading with his.

"And I need to help you."

I sighed and slumped back down on the sofa. "I could call the police."

"But you're not going to."

I rested my head in my hands. "Lord, help me."

"That's what He's trying to do—*through me.*"

"He sent you here to rescue me or something? Is that what you're saying?"

"Maybe… or maybe I'm the one who needs to be rescued."

I bent over and rested my forehead on the arm of the sofa. "I don't like this. I don't like how you—" I cut myself off before adding, "make me feel." But it was the truth, I didn't like how he made me feel at all.

"You don't like how I what?"

I looked up at him towering over me with a look of confusion on his face. "Uh… how you… how you make coffee. You, uh, made it too strong. And you put sugar in it. I take my coffee black."

He scratched the back of his head. "Oh, well, my apologies. You'll have to show me how to make it."

"No, I can do it."

"Okay, are you hungry?"

"Yes, but I can fix something. Are *you* hungry?"

"Yeah. Let me fix us both something. You can barely stand up."

I sighed and decided to give up. "Okay."

14
"Pieces of Me"

I was sitting on the back deck later that day, watching Michael fish from the end of the pier. It was a beautiful day—not too hot, but just right. I sat there for a long time, watching him, wondering about him. Wondering what made him tick, and well, why he was so beautiful. I watched the wind blow through his hair as he sat hunched at the end of the pier, his feet dangling over the water. Even his doggone back was sexy—with clothes *on*. I sighed and crossed my legs and wondered why God would send this man to help me when all I was doing in the process was lusting after him. It just made absolutely no sense to me, and it was downright tortuous to be around him.

I got up, slowly made my way out to the end of the pier, and stood behind him, willing myself not to reach out and brush my hand across his hair as the lake wind blew across his head.

"You wanna sit down?" he asked, startling me.

"Uh…"

He set his pole down, stood to his feet, and helped me down onto the pier. Then he settled back onto his spot.

"Uh, any luck?" I asked.

His eyes were focused on the water. "Not yet."

"How long do you plan on staying out here?"

He glanced over at me and smiled. "Until I catch some fish." He leaned over and submerged his right hand into the lake while gripping the pole with the other hand.

"Are you really Cherokee?" I asked.

"Yes."

"Is that why you like nature and water so much?"

He glanced at me. "What makes you think I like nature and water?"

"Oh… well, the flowers and the way you are now. You seem so at peace out here on the water," I said, silently chiding myself for almost revealing my late-night spying.

"Maybe. My people are all about connecting with, and respecting, nature."

"I see. Um, what do you teach… at the college?"

"The history of the indigenous peoples of the Americas with an emphasis on Cherokee culture, of course. Or, in other words, Native American history. I teach about the customs and languages of my people, including some folklore."

"Really? Sounds interesting. So… you said you're from North Carolina, right? How'd you end up in Arkansas?"

He turned and focused on my face. "I got a teaching job and decided to move. There's nothing left for me in North Carolina. No family, no wife. Everyone… everyone's passed on."

"Oh, I'm… I'm sorry, again… about your wife. Was she Cherokee, too?"

He nodded and refocused on the lake. "Yes. It was—it *is*, uh, very important to me to marry within my race. There are only a few hundred thousand of us left in the United States. I don't suppose I need to tell you why that is."

"Um... no, you don't."

"You know, fish bite a lot better when it's quiet."

I cocked my head to the side. "Is that your way of telling me to shut up?"

He grinned and shook his head. "No, but all of a sudden I feel like I'm on a job interview or something."

I leaned back on my hands and dipped my bare toes in the water. "Well, since you've already spent the night with me, and you refuse to leave, I figured I needed to know at least a little something about you... so that I can describe you to the police."

He laid the fishing pole down on the pier and turned to give me his full attention. "What exactly do you think I would do that would warrant you calling the police?"

I shrugged. "I don't know. *Anything*. Something bad."

"Don't you think that if I really wanted to harm you, I would've by now?"

"I don't know, because *I don't know you*, Michael Ross."

"Hmmm."

"Hmmm?"

He shrugged.

I released an exasperated sigh and then slowly, unsteadily, got to my feet. "I'm leaving, since I'm disturbing the fish."

Before I could take one step back toward the cabin, he jumped up, and after a bit of a struggle, reeled in a huge fish. He laughed loudly. "Ha! You're good luck!"

I rolled my eyes as I walked away.

***

After Michael cleaned the fish, I cut it up and fried it and made us a nice salad to go along with it. Over dinner, he told me about his job in Little Rock, that he'd been teaching there for a year. Before that, he taught classes at a museum in North Carolina.

"So you're big on education, huh?" I asked.

He smiled. "My mother was. She wanted me to get an education and to live well. I guess she was like most parents who want better for their children than they had themselves. She wanted me to have the American dream. My father was all about the tribe and preserving what was left of our culture. I guess they both influenced what I'm doing now in a way. I love learning about many things, and I'm very passionate about sharing the history of my people. I'm working hard to establish a Native American Studies degree program at the university."

I stared at him and wondered to myself if his parents were even half as beautiful as he was. "I see. So you enjoy your work? That's great."

He laid his fork down and leaned back in his chair at the table. "What about you?"

"What about me?"

He grinned. "I think it's time to turn this interrogation around."

I chuckled. "What do you want to know?"

"The picture in the living room, those are your sons?"

"Yes, Derek and Patrick—my pride and joy."

He smiled again. "Great looking boys. What about the rest of your family?"

"Well, my parents still live back in Pine Bluff, and I have one grandparent alive who lives with them, my father's mother. I have a brother who lives in Pine Bluff, too. He's married with four kids. I work at the hospital there as a respiratory therapist, but I'm on leave right now."

"Where are your boys?"

My heart began to race just thinking about Bryan. "With my ex-husband," I said, a slight tremble in my voice.

Michael noticed it. He straightened his posture, his eyes glued to me.

I suddenly lost my appetite. "Um, I think I'm gonna go to bed now. You don't have to stay here. I have your number, and I promise to call if I need anything, but I'm honestly feeling much better now. I'm not nearly as weak and—"

He held up his hand. "Okay, okay. I was planning to spend the night at home anyway. But you be sure to call me if you need me."

"I will, and thanks so much for helping me."

"You're welcome."

After helping me clean up the kitchen, Michael Ross left, and I locked the door behind him. For most of that evening, I sat in the living room and let the TV watch me, and a part of me actually missed Michael's company. I decided I'd better put my mind on something else, so I called my parents.

"Well, hello, stranger. How are things in paradise?" Mama said with a smile in her voice.

I couldn't help but smile, myself. "Hey, Mama. Things are good here. I've been a little under the weather, but my neighbor's been looking out for me."

"Hmm, must be nice to have someone looking out for you."

I fixed my eyes on the bouquet of lavender that sat in a mason jar on the coffee table. "Yes, it is."

"Well, you make sure to thank God for that neighbor when you say your prayers tonight."

"I will. I definitely will. How's everyone there? Grandma Tooley?"

"Me and your daddy are fine. I don't know about Mrs. Tooley. She's still not over this cold. Coughing up a storm and barely eating. I told your daddy that I'm gonna call her doctor again tomorrow and tell him that the medicine he prescribed for her is not working."

"Oh, okay. Well, keep me posted."

"I will, love. Have a good night."

"Okay, good night. Tell Daddy and Grandma I said hi."

"I sure will."

As soon as I hung up with Mama, my phone began to ring. It was Marli.

"Finally!!" she shouted into the phone after I answered it.

"What?" I asked, but I knew she'd probably been trying to reach me. My phone had been dead for almost two days.

"I have been trying to reach you. I was two seconds away from hopping on a plane and coming there to make sure you hadn't disappeared or something."

"Yeah, I'm sorry. My phone was dead. All charged up now."

"Why in the world would you let your phone go dead and stay dead while you're out in the middle of nowhere? What kind of sense does that make, Carla?"

"Damn, *Mom*, I wasn't trying to let it go dead. Something happened, and I just…" I sighed. I wasn't sure if I was ready to tell her what happened.

"What happened? Oh, Lord, did Bryan find you?"

"In a way. I… uh, had a miscarriage yesterday."

"What?! Oh, Carla. I'm sorry. Are you… are you okay?"

I tightly gripped the phone and willed myself not to cry. "It was the rape that did it. I know it was, because I made sure we were careful all of the other times, and I haven't been with another man since St. Louis."

"Carla, I'm so sorry. I really am. Do you need me to come be with you? You shouldn't be alone right now. I'll talk to Chris. I'm sure he won't mind. We can leave the twins with his parents and be on a plane in the morning."

As much as I loved my friend, the last thing I needed to do was witness more of her marital bliss at that moment. "No, I'm okay. Someone is helping me. I'm… I'm good."

"Who's helping you?"

"My neighbor."

"Oh…"

I sighed into the phone. "It's not like that. He's just a very nice person. He feels like he's fulfilling his Christian duty."

"Well, I'm glad God put him so close to you, then. Um, Carla, have you received the package I sent yet?"

"Yes, but I haven't opened it."

"Well, I can understand why since there's so much going on. When you do open it, call me, okay?"

"Okay. I'll talk to you later."

"Okay, bye. Love you, Carla."

"Love you, too, Marli."

I hung up and walked into the kitchen in time to see Michael Ross dive into the lake. I stood and watched him from the window for several minutes before going to bed with a little smile on my face and the thought in my head that I wished I was a Cherokee woman.

15
"What You Do"

I woke up the next morning feeling close to normal. The bleeding had decreased quite a bit, and I didn't feel as weak as I had the day before, so I got up and fixed a nice little breakfast—canned biscuits, bacon, and scrambled eggs. I made a plate, covered it with foil, and walked the few feet to Michael Ross's cabin.

He answered the door after a couple of knocks, and my mouth fell open at the sight of him shirtless, wearing a pair of crisp, white boxers. He leaned against the door frame and said, "Good morning."

I just stood there. Dear God was this man gorgeous! It was like God had taken extra special care in creating him.

"Is that for me?" he asked.

I looked down at the plate in my hand like it was a foreign object, and then my brain reminded me why I was standing at this man's door. I shoved the plate toward him. "Yes, um… good morning."

He took the plate and lifted the foil. "Smells good, thank you."

I clasped my hands in front of me. "Uh, yeah, you're… welcome. I don't know if you eat pork. You're so… so fit and everything."

"I eat it on occasion. I'm sure I'll enjoy it. I was just getting ready to go on my morning run. I'll eat when I come back."

"Oh, okay," I said. Then I just stood there and stared at him.

He eyed me. "You look better."

I gave him a slight smile. "I *feel* better."

"Good. Wanna go for a ride with me later on?"

There was only one ride I was thinking of going on with him, God help me. "A ride?" I said.

"Yes, later on? After lunch?"

"Um, sure."

"Great. See you then."

When he said ride, we were on two different pages. I thought he meant in his truck. Turns out, he meant in his boat, a boat I hadn't even noticed he had. As he helped me into a small, army green boat that reminded me of my late grandfather's fishing boat, I noticed our across the lake neighbors for the first time. Michael climbed in and untied the boat. He grabbed an oar and began to push us away from the shore.

I watched the muscles in his arms flex as he rowed us farther and farther away from land, toward the middle of the lake. Then he stopped, pulled the oar into the boat, and stared out at the water. I stared at him. I watched the wind play with his hair. I observed his strong facial features. I felt his gentle spirit. I wondered if he'd ever laid his hands on his wife like Bryan had me.

"What?" he said, pulling me from my thoughts.

"Huh?" I answered.

"You were staring at me."

If I had been a couple of shades lighter, I swear I would have visibly blushed. "Uh... no, I wasn't. I was looking at the water."

He turned to face me. "No, you were looking at *me*. I felt it."

"Well, you felt *wrong*. Unless you're the lake, I was *not* looking at you." I was actually getting a little heated, like I was telling the truth.

"Hmm," he said.

"What is that supposed to mean?"

"It means, hmm."

I rolled my eyes and muttered, "Whatever." After that, I made it a point *not* to look at him. Or at least I *tried* not to.

He reached down and submerged his hand in the water just as he had the day before.

"Why do you do that?" I asked.

He lifted his hand and scooted closer to me. He smiled and my heart flipped. "Have you always been so curious?"

I shrugged. "I don't know. I guess so."

"Hmm, well, water is life. I like to feel connected to it."

"So when you touch it, you feel connected to it?" I asked.

He nodded and gently took my hand and placed it under the water. "See," he said.

"No," I answered honestly. "It just feels like water to me."

"Close your eyes." He plunged my hand in deeper and held onto it.

I felt something, all right. I felt something in having him so close to me that I could feel his warmth even though the sun was beaming down on us. My heart was racing, and my head was reeling. Being near him was dizzying, and I couldn't understand how a man I'd only known for a short while could make me feel that way.

"Can you feel it?" he whispered.

"Oh, yes, I can," I said.

"Isn't it wonderful?"

I opened my eyes to see him smiling at me. I focused on his lips, licked my own, and said, "Mm-hmm. Yesssss."

He stared at me for a second before releasing my hand. "We'd better be getting back. It's getting kind of hot out here."

Lord knows that's the truth! "Yes. It is."

Michael invited me to his cabin for dinner, and for some crazy reason, I was excited about it. I felt like I was back in high school, crushing over some boy with whom I knew I had no chance. I wasn't Cherokee. As far as I knew, I was 1000% black, and he'd made it clear that he wanted to further his own race. But that didn't stop me from ogling him or fantasizing about him. Actually, lusting after him kept me from thinking about my problems. He was my escape route.

He came and walked me to his place later that evening. Once inside, I found it to be moderately decorated and surmised that the décor had probably already been there when he arrived. There was nothing in that cabin that told me anything about Michael Ross, except for several books that were scattered about the coffee table in the living room and a lone, framed photograph that sat on the mantle.

As I sat down and eyed my surroundings, Michael ducked into the kitchen to check on dinner. I stared at the photo across the room, at a slightly younger Michael embracing a striking woman with flowing hair and a bright smile. I knew she must've been his wife. She was very thin, but she was absolutely beautiful.

He walked back into the living room, hovering near the doorway. "I met her while working on my master's degree. She was actually one of my professors. She was bright and beautiful, and I fell in love with her at first sight." He eased into the room and sat at the opposite end of the couch, his eyes fixed on the photo. "She was older and wiser than me, and I learned a lot from her about my people and about myself."

"What did she teach you about yourself?" I asked.

He rested his arm on the back of the couch and shifted his eyes to me. "I always wanted children, lots of children to keep the bloodlines flowing. Linda taught me that I was willing to sacrifice what I wanted for what I needed. I needed her. I needed to love her. She was too sick to carry children, and I knew that from the beginning, but I still married her, because I loved her. I also learned that I could love another person enough to let them go. I loved her enough to want her suffering to end."

"What was... what was wrong with her?"

He sighed deeply. "She had a lot of chronic health issues. We were married for two years, three months, and four days before they overtook her, and she died."

"You miss her."

"More some days, less others, but yes, I do miss her. Since she's been gone, I've felt like a wanderer, you know? Like a man without a home. She was my home. In a way, I feel homeless, sometimes. I have friends, *good* friends, and great colleagues, but I can be in a room full of people and still feel alone without her."

I clasped my hands in my lap. "I bet you never did anything to hurt her."

"I hope I didn't."

I dropped my eyes and then looked back up at him. "Would you... have you ever hit a woman?"

He frowned. "Never have. Never will. I don't understand men that do."

"Neither do I. I don't understand how a person can love someone and hurt them at the same time. I don't see how that's even possible, but I guess it is."

He shook his head. "No, it isn't. You can't truly love someone and hurt them like that. To love someone is to respect them and to protect them, not hurt them."

"I guess you're right. Do you think you'll ever marry again?"

"I can't say. Who knows? Maybe God has another Chero—another woman out there for me."

"Maybe."

We were both quiet for a couple of minutes. Michael broke into the silence with, "You hungry? Dinner's ready."

Dinner was grilled meatloaf with mashed cauliflower and a nice kale salad, which, he confessed, came from a local restaurant.

"What were you 'checking on' in the kitchen earlier, then?" I asked.

"The microwave," he said with a wink, and then he laughed.

I laughed, too.

With a twinkle in his eye, he asked, "How's the food?"

"It's good. Never had mashed cauliflower before."

"Yeah, it's a good alternative to mashed potatoes. Tasty, minus all of the carbs."

"I see."

"How long were you married?" he asked, almost making me choke on the sip of water I'd just taken.

"Uh-technically, a little more than fifteen years."

"*Technically?*"

"We were separated for four years before we finalized our divorce."

"You tried to make it work?"

"Yeah." I pushed my plate away. "I don't—can we change the subject?"

He slowly nodded. "Sure. Tell me about your boys."

I grinned at the mention of my babies. "Sure, but, uh… can we go back into the living room?"

"Yeah. You're done?"

"Yeah, uh… I wasn't that hungry."

"Okay, let me make some coffee real quick. You want some? I promise not to make it too strong or put sugar in it."

I nodded and gave him another smile. "I'd love some."

We settled into the living room, and I told him about my boys, their love of video games, and their appetites that I couldn't seem to keep enough food in my kitchen to satisfy.

He chuckled. "Well, that's how boys are. In the old days, in my people's culture, they would already be learning to hunt and fish.

They would need the food for energy."

I glanced at the books on the table. "Are all of these books about Native American-uh, indigenous peoples' culture?"

He nodded. "Yes, and some of them are just about American history. It's hard to find books that tell the story straight without demonizing my people, but I've found a few."

"Yeah, I haven't read much about your people, but I've seen how they're portrayed in movies—"

"Like savages, wild men, when all they were trying to do was defend their land and their lives. Killing is wrong, I'm not condoning that, but they felt pushed into it."

I nodded. "I know."

"Heavy talk, huh?"

I shrugged. "I guess, but it's the truth."

There was a moment of slightly awkward silence before I said, "You said you teach folklore?"

"Yes."

"Can you tell me a story?"

He leaned back and gazed toward the ceiling. "Hmm, I guess I can tell you a quick one. How about *The Legend of the First Woman?*"

I leaned against the back of the couch and gave him a little smile. "Okay."

He scooted a little closer to my end of the couch and fixed his eyes on me. "In the beginning of time, man was very happy on the earth—roaming around exploring, enjoying the fruits and berries, visiting the animals. Then he became dissatisfied and unhappy, but he had no idea what was wrong with him. You know what his problem was?"

I shook my head, never taking my eyes off of him. "No."

"He was *bored*. And because he was bored, he began to behave differently. He would slaughter a deer that he didn't need, or pick a plant and not use it. He became destructive, too. He destroyed the animals' dens just to entertain himself. And the animals became concerned."

His voice was soft as he scooted to the edge of the couch and continued. "Well, the animals called a meeting to try to figure out what to do. They were all surprised at his actions, because he had a mind and was supposed to respect all of the other creatures. So, after great discussion, they called on the man's maker—the Great One. They told him all that the man had been doing, his new destructive ways. And the Great One was thankful that they'd told him these things. He realized he'd left something out when he made the man."

"What?" I asked softly, feeling like a school girl listening to her gorgeous, magnetic teacher tell a story.

He brushed a piece of his hair from his brow with his fingers and said, "Well, he made a green plant grow tall." He raised his hand for emphasis. "The plant grew right over the man's heart. It had long, elegant leaves and an ear of corn and a golden braid. Directly above the tall plant was a woman. A lovely, *brown* woman was growing from a stalk of corn.

"The man woke up, and he couldn't believe his eyes! He thought he was dreaming until the Great One explained to him that he was to be her man. There's a little more to the story involving the significance of corn to my people. But you get the gist of it."

I nodded. "Do you believe that story?"

He smiled. "I believe that God made woman for man. And I believe that without woman, man is truly lost."

I returned his smile and forced myself to stop staring at him. Instead, I stared at the coffee table.

"You like music?" he asked, startling me a little.

"Huh? Oh, yes, I do."

"What's your favorite song?"

"Um… 'Umbrella' by Rihanna."

"Okay, that's a pretty good choice."

I tilted my head to the side and raised an eyebrow. "Pretty good? It's a great song! What kind of music do you listen to?"

"I like foreign music, international music. I have a ton of Putamayo CD's. And I like Native American music, too."

"Okay, what's *your* favorite song?"

"'Tous Les Jours Tous Les Soirs' by Monsieur Nov."

"Um, what?"

He chuckled. "He's a French R&B singer."

"For real?"

"Yep. Hold on a second." He left the living room and returned with his phone. I watched as he swiped the screen a few times, then a song began to play. It was a slow groove, and the singer delivered the lyrics so sensually, I had to adjust in my seat and cross my legs. It didn't help that Michael was sitting across from me looking finer than I thought was humanly possible, with his eyes closed, nodding his head to the music.

I cleared my throat, and his eyes popped open and settled on me. "It really is a nice song," I said. "Um, do you understand what he's saying?"

He nodded. "He's seducing her, telling her what she can expect from him, uh, in the bedroom."

I uncrossed and re-crossed my legs. "Hmm, I didn't know you knew French."

"I know a little."

I wiped my forehead and glanced nervously around the room. "Man, it's warm in here."

Michael frowned and glanced at the fireplace. "You want me to kill the fire? Is it burning too high?"

If only he knew the double meaning in his statement. "No, uh... I think I'm just getting tired. I should probably go now."

"Well, let me walk you back home. I guess it *is* getting late."

"Yeah, um, thanks for dinner."

He smiled. "You're welcome."

He walked me home, and I rushed into the bathroom and took a cold shower. Then I waited up until after midnight to watch him skinny dip. When sleep finally overtook me, Michael still had not taken his nightly dip in the lake. But he inhabited every second of my dreams.

16

"Goin' Thru Changes"

When I woke up the next morning, Michael's truck was already gone, so I fixed just enough breakfast for myself. After eating and calling to check on the boys, I settled down in the living room and finally opened the package from Marli. Inside was a small journal and several printed internet pages and pamphlets from the RAINN (Rape, Abuse, and Incest National Network) website. I had visited the website a few times and read some of the information, but I just didn't think any of it applied to me. I knew I'd been raped, but not like *regular* rape. What happened with Bryan was different. It was... complicated, and I didn't think anything on those sheets of paper would benefit me. But I appreciated Marli for trying to help. I decided I would call her later and thank her.

I checked Michael's driveway off and on throughout the day to see if he'd returned home. When it began to get dark, I decided to sit on the porch so that I could see him pull up. I kind of missed his company, or maybe I just missed looking at him or being around him. Goodness just seemed to ooze from his pores, and I felt safe with him. As soon as I stepped out onto the porch, I felt the familiar sensation of flowers crushing beneath my bare feet. I smiled as I bent over and picked up the bouquet of fragrant, purple flowers and held it up to my nose.

I clutched the flowers in my hand and took a seat on the wooden glider swing that sat on the porch. I gently swayed back and forth, a faint smile on my face as I thought about Michael Ross and his smile and the powerful arms that had helped me into the house when I got home from the hospital. I thought about his hands, the smooth, hairless skin of his chest, and then I told myself to stop. This was crazy. I hadn't known him long enough to be sitting there fantasizing and yearning. It was just ridiculous for a woman my age—damn near forty—with two half-grown sons to be acting the way I was acting. I was almost ashamed of myself, but who could blame me? The man was, hands down, the single most gorgeous male creature I'd ever laid eyes on.

"Sorry, Marli, but Michael's got Chris beat," I whispered to myself. Then I began to giggle, and I'm not a giggler. A minute or so later, my giggle turned into a full-on belly laugh with tears. Seconds later, the tears of laughter transformed into tears of sorrow.

I held the flowers to my chest and cried with an ache from deep inside of me. I doubled over and moaned and sobbed until my head hurt, and I thought surely I would run out of tears, but I didn't. It was as if at that very moment, I fully realized what was going on in my life. I'd lost a husband, a marriage, and a baby in just a few months' time, and suddenly, I felt hollow inside.

"Why?" I wailed as I tightly shut my eyes and rocked back and forth. "*Why?*"

I would be the first to admit that I'd done my dirt. I'd had so many anonymous and known sexual encounters in St. Louis, it'd make a porn star blush. Maybe this was my punishment for my adultery since, after all, I was still married at the time. And though Bryan cheated first, everyone knows that two wrongs don't make a right. I lost myself back then. I lost all of my common sense. I lost my faith, too, and I still hadn't found it.

When I opened my eyes and lifted my head, Michael Ross was standing at the foot of my porch with a frown on his face. I quickly wiped my wet cheeks and rubbed my hand over my braided hair.

"How... how long have you been standing there?" I asked.

"Long enough."

I swiped at my nose. "Where've you been?" I asked before I could stop myself. What was wrong with me?

He stepped onto the bottom step. "I had an appointment. Did you need me for something?"

I straightened my posture and squared my shoulders. "No."

He stepped up onto the next step. "Then why'd you ask?"

"I don't... I was just wondering."

"Have you eaten?" he asked as he stepped up onto the porch and towered over me.

"Of course I have," I said with a bit of a bite. I wasn't even sure what I was mad about. Him catching me crying? Him being gone? Me caring?

"Okay," he said. "Do you need anything?"

"No, I was just gonna go inside and lie down."

"Let me help you—"

"No!" I closed my eyes and shook my head. "No, thank you."

He stood there, staring down at me with those damn eyes that made every nerve in my body stand at attention. He just stared at me. Then he turned and left without another word.

I stomped into my cabin, locked the door behind me, and climbed into bed without even bothering to eat dinner.

***

The next morning, I was on the phone with my mother while sitting on the front porch, my eyes glued to Michael's cabin. Again, he was already gone, but when I stepped out onto the porch this time, no flowers greeted me. As Mama gave me an update on Grandma Tooley, who sounded like she was getting worse instead of better, I realized that I hadn't thought to thank Michael for the flowers the day before. I was too busy being angry at him for no reason to think to do it. I decided that whenever he made it back home, I'd apologize for my behavior. Maybe I'd even cook dinner for him.

"Carla Sue, are you still there?" Mama asked.

"Uh, yes, ma'am. What'd you say?"

"I said, I think I'ma take Ms. Tooley on to the urgent care clinic today since it's Saturday, and the doctor's office is closed."

"Yes, ma'am, you say she's wheezing?"

"Mm-hmm. And still coughing up a storm."

"Yeah, you'd better take her in. This has been going on too long for it just to be a cold. I know you said she was having trouble swallowing. I hope she hasn't aspirated on some food."

"Aspa-what?"

"That's a term for when something gets into the lungs that's not supposed to be there, like food that doesn't get swallowed correctly."

"Oh... well, Lord, I hope that's not what's going on."

"I hope it's not, either. I wish I was there to check her out. I can come back if you need me to."

"No, no, I'ma take her on to the clinic and see what they say. No sense in you driving all the way back here when the clinic is so close."

"Okay." I stared at Michael's empty driveway. "Mama, you think there's such a thing as love at first sight?"

"I suppose anything's possible. Why you ask?"

"No reason. Um, I'll let you go so you can get Grandma Tooley to the clinic. Let me know how it goes."

"All right. Bye, baby."

I sighed as I ended the call and headed back into the house.

17

"Unsaid"

For two more days, Michael Ross came and went like a ghost. I never saw when he made it home, and by the time I realized he was there, he was leaving again. Okay, I can admit that my feelings were a little hurt. I thought we were on our way to being friends. All right, who the hell was I kidding? I had a thing for him. A strange, inexplicable connection to this tall man with the thick, black hair and piercing, brown eyes. I felt like I was a tween, and the boy I had a crush on had been absent from school. I actually felt like a lunatic, because it made no sense for me to be virtually stalking a man I'd only kind of, sort of known for a couple of weeks. What was I going to do when I went back home? Find someone else to stalk? I shook my head at my own thoughts as I stood there and stared out the kitchen window at the lake that my neighbor hadn't skinny dipped in for days.

 I walked out onto the back deck and was just about to sit down when my cell phone rang. I rushed into the living room, thinking that it might be my mother calling. The doctor at the clinic had diagnosed Grandma Tooley with aspiration pneumonia, just as I'd feared, and she didn't seem to be getting any better. He was trying to avoid admitting her to the hospital, but that was a strong possibility at her age. I was on alert in case I needed to return home. But to my surprise, the call was not from my mother. The number flashing on my screen belonged to my son's cell phone.

 I answered it, stepped back out onto the deck, and took a seat in one of the patio chairs. "Hey, Derek?"

"Yes, ma'am."

Something in his voice caught my immediate attention. He didn't sound quite right. "Derek, what's going on? Is something wrong?"

"No-yes, ma'am."

I sprang up from my seat. "What is it?"

"Um, Daddy brought us over here to Grandma Tina's house like three days ago, and he ain't came back to pick us up."

I frowned as I leaned against the outer wall of the cabin. "What? Why'd he take you over there?"

I could almost hear Derek shrug through the phone. "I'on know. Usually, me and Patrick just stay at the house by ourselves when he goes to work, but this time, he brought us over here. We ready to go, Mama. It smells over here, and she ain't got no good cable channels. We're bored."

I almost laughed, because I knew the smell he was referring to was mothballs. That place smelled like Bryan's mother had mothballs hidden in every corner. "Um, let me see if I can get your dad and find out what's going on."

"I tried to call him, but he ain't answering."

"Well, I'll try anyway. If I can't get him, I'll see what else I can do." I hung up the phone and thought to myself that maybe I should go back home. Maybe I'd had enough time away. But as I dialed Bryan's number, and the feelings of dread and anxiety that my mind always associated with talking to him rose back up, I decided that maybe I wasn't ready to go back after all. Bryan's phone went straight to voicemail, so I hung up and dialed his number again. This time it rang, almost as if he'd had it off and had just turned it back on.

"Hello?" his painfully familiar voice answered.

"Bryan, it's Carla. What's going on with the boys?"

"I knew it was you."

I sighed in frustration. Leave it to him to only address part of what I said—the unimportant part. "What's going on with the boys, Bryan?"

"What are you talking about? The boys are fine. They're at my mom's."

"I know that. Derek just called me. They're tired of being over there. You know your mom's house isn't equipped to entertain kids."

He chuckled bitterly. "You never did like my mother, did you? Why are you calling me trying to start some mess over the boys? This is *my* six weeks with them, and what I do with them and where I take them is none of your business!"

I began to pace the deck floor. Bryan had crawled under my skin and pitched a tent. If there was one thing I couldn't stand, it was someone talking trash to me about my babies, and Bryan knew that. He knew it *well*. I was so upset, I didn't even hear Michael pull into his driveway.

"I don't know what hole you just crawled out of that's got you thinking you can talk to me like that," I said. "But you better crawl back in there and get your mind right. *Everything* that happens concerning my boys is my business. Things have been good between us, Bryan, despite the stuff that happened in the past. But if you ever make the mistake of thinking that you can talk to me like that about my own sons again, things are gonna get ugly!"

"How can they get any uglier than you blackmailing me, Carla? Fifteen years of marriage, and I never stopped loving you, and you blackmail me into a divorce? I can't believe you could be that lowdown!"

"Well, if you weren't so busy being hugged up with your married, down-low, deacon lover, you would've noticed me, and I wouldn't have been able to take those pictures! Is that where you've been? With *him*? Is that why you've had my boys over at your mama's house inhaling mothball fumes for *three freakin' days?!* If so, you need to schedule your little booty calls for when my sons are not with you!"

"You're talking big now, huh? But the last few times I saw you, you were running away from me. All because I took what the hell was, *and always will be,* mine."

I stopped pacing, and my hand began to tremble. I opened my mouth to speak, but couldn't.

"Yeah, where's all of that big talk *now*? Where are you? You still visiting your friend? I'll come take it again if I want to, and there ain't a thing you can do but let me!"

My entire body began to shake. "I'll kill you before I let you hurt me again. Now, you need to get over to your mama's house and get my boys. They better not have to call me again about this."

I ended the call and tightly gripped the phone in my hand while releasing a ragged breath. Had he really just threatened to rape me again? I stood there and stared at... nothing. I just stared. What had kept me from going completely over the edge was the belief that Bryan hadn't really meant to rape me, that it all happened in the heat of the moment. But the words he'd just said to me told me otherwise. They told me that he was well aware of what he'd done and that he was more than willing to do it again.

"Hey, you all right?"

I nearly jumped from the deck, over the pier, and into the lake. I stared at Michael, too disturbed to be relieved to see him.

"Carla, *are you all right?*" he repeated.

I wanted to lie. I wanted to put on a brave front and nod my head and walk into my house all cool, calm, and collected. But standing before me was the only tangible source of comfort I'd had in a long time. So I lowered my head, allowed my tears to flow, and said, "No."

Michael, who was standing in the yard next to the deck, made use of his long legs and climbed onto the deck from the side, without using the steps. In seconds, he was holding my crumpled body as I cried into his chest.

***

I rolled over on the sofa to find Michael Ross sitting in a chair across from me, reading something. I smiled. There was no need in pretending I didn't want him there, and I wouldn't bother asking him to leave, because every part of me wanted him to stay.

"How long was I asleep?" I asked as I stretched my arms over my head.

"A couple of hours," he said, his eyes glued to whatever he was reading.

I sat up and tried to get a better look at what had his attention. "What are you reading?"

He looked up at me, hesitantly leaned across the coffee table, and handed the papers to me. It was the information that Marli had sent me from RAINN. My chest tightened. I looked up at Michael and then back down at the papers.

"They were just lying on the table," he said.

I placed them back on the table, laying them facedown.

"Did someone rape you?" he asked as he leaned forward and looked me in the eye.

I stared back at him. "Not really."

He raised an eyebrow and sat back in his chair a bit. "What does that mean? Either someone did, or they didn't."

"I... think so."

"You think so? Carla, what happened to you? Something is obviously wrong."

I sighed and closed my eyes. "Michael, this is too heavy for you. You don't know me like that."

"That's how you got pregnant, isn't it?"

I shook my head.

"Yes, it is. Who raped you?"

Something in his voice had changed. I opened my eyes. "It doesn't matter. I don't think it really was a rape."

"Who were you talking to on the phone?"

"Uh, that's none of your business. Thank you for helping me, Michael, but you should probably go now."

He stood from his chair and nodded. "I'm being dismissed again, huh?"

I looked up at him with wide eyes. "What are you talking about? I'm not dismissing you, but you're asking a bunch of questions that I can't answer right now."

"I have asked God why in the world He wants me to help someone who doesn't want my help. I'm still waiting on an answer."

"I *do* want your help. It's just hard for me. It's hard to talk about it."

He threw up his hands. "Just tell me. All I want to do is help you. *Just tell me.*"

"I can't."

He walked over to the sofa and squatted down next to me. "Who raped you, Carla? All I want to do is help you. Tell me who did it."

I stared at him, at the compassion in his eyes, and right then, I realized something about him, something that made me feel like I could share my darkest secrets with him. I realized that he really cared about me. Tears raced down my face as I held my head in my hands. "My ex-husband did it, but he was still my husband at the time. He-he raped me, and I'm so scared… I'm scared he's going to do it again."

I buried my face in my hands and continued to cry. A second later, I felt Michael pull my hands from my face, wipe my tears with his palms, and gather me into his arms.

18
"Lost and Found (Find Me)"

We sat in silence in my living room—Michael's eyes on me, my eyes on the floor. I'd told him everything from Bryan's infidelity, to the rape, to the phone call we'd had earlier and Bryan's veiled threat to violate me again.

"I'm just glad he doesn't know where I am right now," I said.

"Why didn't you have him arrested?" Michael asked.

I looked at him. "At first, I was trying to protect my sons. Bryan's a good father, and I didn't want my sons to know what had happened. I knew it would destroy them. Then, as time passed, I think I was just afraid that no one would believe me. I mean, after all, he *was* my husband. He was entitled to have sex with me."

He leaned forward. "He was not entitled to hit you or to force you to do *anything*. You should've called the police. He is *not* a good father, Carla. A good father respects the mother of his children."

I shook my head. "You don't know him. He's... he's not a bad person. He just... he was upset."

"Didn't you say that he just threatened to hurt you again? Sounds like a bad person to me."

"I provoked him."

"My wife could never have provoked me into harming her."

I didn't have a rebuttal for that, so I just sat there and stared at the floor again.

"Will you make a promise to me and to yourself?" he asked.

"What?"

"That if he ever tries to hurt you again, you will call the police?"

I hesitated, then nodded. "I promise."

"Good. As long as you're here, I'll protect you."

"That's okay; like I said, he doesn't even know where I am."

"What'll you do when you go back home?"

I sighed. "I have no idea."

"You should get a restraining order."

"But my boys… I don't want to disrupt their lives."

Michael shook his head. "He is not a good father, and you can't be a good mother if you're living in fear all of the time."

I leaned against the back of the couch. He was right, and I knew it. At that point, I really didn't know how to handle things. I just didn't know what to do. "Michael…"

He raised a hand. "I'm not gonna push you. Just think about it."

"I will."

"You hungry?"

"Actually, no. I've lost my appetite."

"Well, you need to eat." He stood, walked over to me, and offered me his hand. "You okay to walk a little bit?"

I took his hand, noticed that his wedding band was missing, wondered when and why he took it off. "Well, yes... I guess so. Where are we going?"

"You'll see. I just need to get something out of my cabin first."

We left my cabin and stopped by his. I waited out on his porch for a few minutes, and when he came back outside, he hoisted a backpack onto his back and took my hand in his. He led me from the cabin out to the dirt road, and we walked along the road in silence, my hand in his. It was a peaceful walk—hot, but peaceful. He stopped and I looked up at him. "We need to cut through the woods here," he said.

I frowned slightly. "I thought you said we were just walking a little bit."

"It's not far."

"What's not far?"

"You'll see."

"If I get weak, you'll have to carry me."

He gazed down at me, and my heart skipped four or five beats. "That won't be a problem," he said. He pulled on my hand, but I didn't move.

"Are there any snakes in there?" I asked.

He grinned. "Why? Are you afraid of snakes?"

"No, I'm afraid of being bitten by one."

He tugged on my hand again. "Come on. I jog through here every morning, never seen a snake."

I resisted. "There's a first time for everything."

He leaned in close to me. "I promise to protect you."

His closeness was unnerving and intoxicating at the same time. I stared into his eyes and nodded. "Okay."

We walked through the woods for so long that I felt like I was in a low budget version of *Lord of the Rings,* except there was no magic ring, and hopefully, there were no Orcs around, either. I was just about to tell him I wanted to go back to my cabin when we made it to a clearing—a field of what looked like miles of lavender.

I smiled and looked up at Michael. "It's so beautiful!"

He returned my smile. "Yes, it is."

He released my hand, dropped his backpack, and unzipped it, pulling out a blanket. I stood to the side as he spread the blanket on the ground next to the bed of lavender. Then he pulled out a big covered bowl and two plastic forks. He took my hand and helped me down onto the blanket, and then he sat down beside me and pulled the top off of the bowl to reveal a beautiful fruit salad.

"I figured since you said you're not very hungry, we could eat light," he said as he handed me a fork.

"Thank you. It looks good."

As he plunged his fork into the bowl, I asked, "Um… did you bring any small bowls?"

He speared a piece of cantaloupe with his fork and shoved it into his mouth. "Nope. We don't need bowls. We can share this one."

I frowned at him as he popped another piece of fruit into his mouth. "Is this sanitary?"

He shrugged. "I don't know."

I sat there, fork in hand, eyeing the fruit as he continued to eat.

My stomach grumbled, and I sighed, closed my eyes, and said a quick grace. Then I dug into the bowl.

Michael smiled. "Good, huh?"

I nodded. "Yeah."

I ate until I was fuller than I thought a person could get from eating fruit, then we sat quietly beside each other, observing the nature surrounding us. Michael leaned back on his hands and faced the sky with his eyes closed and a smile on his face. I smiled, too, as I watched him. I had never wanted to touch another human being as badly as I wanted to touch Michael Ross at that moment. I wanted to comb my fingers through his hair and kiss his lips. When he opened his eyes and looked over at me, I jumped and dropped my eyes.

"I love it out here," he said. "I could sit here like this for the rest of the day."

"I bet. You need a ranch or a farm or something, huh?" I said.

"That's one of my dreams—to have a ranch with lots of land, raw land that I can explore. What do *you* dream about?"

Other than you? I shrugged. "Nothing."

He frowned. "You don't have dreams?"

I pulled my knees up and rested my chin on them. "I used to dream of having a big house with nice furniture and lots of money in the bank. Well, I had all of that, and it didn't keep my marriage from falling apart. I don't have any dreams left."

"Yes, you do. You just have to find them."

"Hmm, I don't know if I even *want* to dream anymore."

"Why not?"

"I don't have any faith in dreams anymore. I don't have much faith in *anything* anymore. I think I've lost my religion or something. Haven't been to church since I found my husband laid up with an active deacon. I'm just all messed up. My life is a hot mess."

"You can miss church and still keep your faith. I know church is important, but it's not a necessity for worship. I worship God all the time."

With a slightly furrowed brow, I said, "Really?"

He rolled over and faced me. "Yes! For instance, if I see something beautiful, I will look at it for a long time, study it. And then I'll look up to Heaven." He turned his head to demonstrate. "And I'll either talk to God in my heart, or I'll say the words: 'Father, thank You for Your creations. Thank You for Your love. Thank You for Your grace.'" He rolled back over and looked at me again.

"That's beautiful, Michael. Maybe I'll try that. Um, your people weren't traditionally Christians, were they?" I asked.

"No. not originally. Christianity is a religion that the white man brought to them."

"How do you reconcile that? I mean, you say you want to remain true to your people. How can you do that if you don't adopt their religion?"

"I don't consider Christianity just a religion. It's a way of life. I believe in God because I *know* Him. I believe that, in their own way, my ancestors believed in God, too. What about you? How do you reconcile being a Christian with the way your ancestors worshipped?"

I shrugged. "I don't know anything about my ancestors. I have no idea where they were from, though I assume it was somewhere in

Africa."

"You should find out. It's important for us to know where we came from. Our ancestors are a part of us."

I nodded and shifted my attention to the field of flowers. "They really are beautiful."

"Yes, they are."

I sat there for a moment, looking at the flowers and trying not to look at Michael. But he was like a lure to me, and I found myself glancing at him over and over again as he lay there with his eyes closed and a slight smile on his face. I looked up to Heaven and thought, *Thank You, God, for creating this beautiful man—even if I can't have him.* Then I laid on my back and let the sun bathe my face.

19

"Better"

I wasn't sure how long I slept, but when my eyes opened, the sky was darker; the sunlight had dissipated quite a bit. I turned my head and looked at Michael, who was lying on his side, staring at me.

"How long was I asleep?" I asked as I rolled over to face him.

"A little longer than I was."

"That's not answering my question."

He smiled. "I know." He reached over and rested his hand on my cheek, and my heart began to beat so rapidly, it was as if it was chasing something. In an instant, everything around us fell silent. The noises of nature were muted for a few seconds, and when the sounds returned, they were heightened. I could almost hear an ant stepping onto a leaf, or the sound of a bird's wings flapping from high in the sky. I opened my mouth to say something, but my mind went blank, and instead, I rested my cheek in his hand and closed my eyes. I could feel him moving closer to me, but I didn't open my eyes, because the tenderness of his touch had caused them to well up, and I didn't want to cry—not at that moment.

When his lips met mine, I thought I would melt into a puddle of Carla right then and there. He kissed me with a mixture of gentleness and a passion that I'd never experienced before. Yet, in some strange way, his lips felt familiar. Maybe that was because I'd felt his kisses in my dreams. I combed my fingers through his thick, coarse hair as I returned the kiss with an equal measure of passion. If he didn't know I wanted him before that moment, I'd done my best to tell him with that kiss. The kiss lingered on as he rubbed his huge hands up and down my back, pulling me closer and closer to him. I could've kissed that man for hours and still not have been satisfied.

When he released me, he stared into my eyes, and I stared right back. I loved looking at him, but just looking wasn't enough anymore—not after having tasted his lips. I moved in, threaded my fingers through his thick hair again, and covered his lips with mine. This time, he was less gentle and more urgent with his half of the kiss. We kissed for a very long time, only coming up for air for a brief moment. We would've stayed there in that field, kissing and touching each other, all night long had a clap of thunder not shaken us apart. Now I knew why the sky looked so dark. There was a storm brewing.

"We should head back," he said breathily.

"Yeah, we should," I agreed.

We packed up our picnic and held hands as we navigated our way through the woods back to our cabins, both of us smiling widely. I even caught myself giggling like a schoolgirl a couple of times. Then the ceiling fell out of the sky, and the rain began to pour all at once. I yelped and tried to make a run for it, but Michael held on to my hand.

"Wait," he said. He dropped my hand and held his head back, letting the downpour flood his face. "Thank You, God, for the rain!" he shouted. Then he let out a loud, "Whoop!"

I stood there and tried to forget about the expensive weave that was braided into my hair, because I didn't want to leave him. I never wanted us to be apart. So I closed my eyes and let the rain bathe me, too. I faced the sky, spread my arms, and whispered, "Thank You, God, for today. Thank You for sending this man to me." I stood there for a moment before feeling Michael's arms slip around my waist, and there we were, two rain-soaked bodies, embracing, lips locked, and my only thought was that I loved him. I knew that as well as I knew my own name. It didn't matter how long or short a time I'd known him. I loved him. And his kisses told me that he loved me, too.

***

We walked into my cabin hand-in-hand, both of us laughing as our shoes squished on the hardwood floor. Michael dropped the water-logged backpack and swept me into his arms. We'd kissed and held each other off and on throughout the walk back, and it seemed that we still couldn't get enough of each other.

When he finally released me, he said, "I'm gonna go to my place and change into something dry. Um, you want to come over for a real dinner, or maybe we could go to a restaurant?" He smiled as he traced my eyebrow with his fingertip.

"Sure. A real dinner at your place sounds good."

He leaned in and gently brushed my lips with his. "See you in a few."

I smiled. "Okay."

After he left, I danced into my bedroom to find a change of clothes. I took a quick shower, dressed, and decided to check my cell phone to delay going to Michael's cabin. I didn't want to seem too eager, although I wanted to sprint the few feet from my cabin to his and fall right into his arms.

I called to check on my sons, who were both doing fine, and

Grandma Tooley, who was doing about the same. Then I sat on the side of the bed and smiled at my reflection in the dresser mirror. *Lord, you are something else*, I thought. *Just when I decide to swear off men, you send me to live right next to one and make him so wonderful that I almost fall in love with him the first time I see him.* I giggled lightly as I checked the time. It was time for me to head over to Michael's.

We had a nice dinner at his place, and afterwards, we sat in front of a lit fireplace and talked about everything and nothing in particular. When we ran out of words, we just sat there, his fingers laced through mine as he rubbed his other hand across my water-damaged braids.

"I'll have to take these out now, since they got so wet," I said.

"Oh... sorry," he replied.

"It's okay. It was probably time to take them out anyway." I reached up and touched his damp hair. "I wonder how you look with longer hair."

He grinned. "Hmm, I look like me... with longer hair."

I rolled my eyes. "*Duh*, I mean I'd like to see it for myself."

He leaned in and softly kissed me. "Then I'll let it grow."

"You will?"

"For you I will."

I sighed as I leaned against him, resting my head on his shoulder. "I never want to leave this place, this lake. This place brought me back to life. I was dying before I came here."

"Then don't leave."

I glanced up at him. "My life is not here, Michael."

"It could be. We could buy one of the cabins and be together—me, you, and your boys."

"My boys don't know you, and they've been through a lot already this year. I'd hate to uproot them."

He wrapped his arm around me. "Then I'll come to you."

I sat up and looked him in the eye. "You'd do that? You'd move to Pine Bluff for me? But I'm... I'm *not* Cherokee. I'm black."

"Didn't you say that Pine Bluff is close to Little Rock? I could commute. And I'm well aware of your race, Carla."

"It doesn't matter to you anymore? I mean, you seemed to have such strong convictions about furthering your race."

He leaned in and kissed me deeply. "What I feel for you is much, *much* stronger. My heart needs to be near you. You've taught me that race doesn't matter, that love is stronger than any conviction I might have. Thank you."

"But I thought..."

"You thought what?"

"That you weren't over your wife."

"Carla, I miss her from time to time, but she's gone. You're here, and *I love you*. I feel alive again because of you. I want to be with *you*."

"W-well, what are we gonna do? Where will you live if you come to Pine Bluff?"

He shrugged. "I can get my own place until we're ready to get married."

I shifted my eyes to the fireplace. I wanted to be with him, but the rational part of my mind had suddenly kicked in, and it was screaming at me, telling me that things were moving too fast, that there was no way this would work.

"I won't let you go back there alone and risk your ex-husband hurting you again," he said.

"Michael… I don't know. Maybe this is too much too soon. We haven't known each other long, and you're already talking about marriage."

"*Eventually*. Not today. Look, I love you, Carla. I've known that for a while now—since the moment I laid eyes on you, really. I think you feel the same way about me."

"I do. I think I've known it for a while, too."

"Did you know it when you used to watch me swim?"

My mouth dropped open. "*You knew?* All this time, you knew?"

He laughed. "I knew from the first time. I saw you sitting out there on your deck."

"Why didn't you say anything?"

"Because I liked that you were watching me."

"You're an exhibitionist!"

"And you're a voyeur."

"No, I'm not!"

"Yes, you are, but I like that about you."

He leaned in and kissed me, and I kissed him right back.

20

"Golden"

The next morning, I woke up to persistent knocks at my back door. I smiled as I wrapped my robe around my body. I knew it was probably Michael, and I wasn't even mad about him waking me up from my sleep. The way he had me feeling, he could've knocked on my door at 1:00 A.M., and I would've still been grinning from ear to ear.

"Good morning, beautiful," he said as he slid past me, pressing a soft kiss on my cheek as I shut the door behind him.

"Good morning," I replied.

"Are you busy today?"

I shook my head. "Not at all."

He smiled. "Good. I want to show you something."

"Okay. What?"

"It's a surprise. Just dress comfortably. I'll pick you up in an hour," he said, then he planted a lingering kiss on my lips.

I wrapped my arms around his neck and returned his kiss. I honestly could have stood there locked in his arms with our lips connected indefinitely, and I would not have minded at all. When we finally parted, I caught my breath and whispered, "I'll be ready."

He rubbed the back of his hand across my cheek. "I can't wait."

I rushed to the shower, threw on a peach-colored, floral, cami sundress and some comfortable sandals, and slid on my favorite lip gloss. It was hot, and if there was any chance of us being outside, a full face of make-up would be ruined. Au natural seemed to be the way to go. I sprayed on a little Bath and Body Works Japanese Cherry Blossom and sat in my living room, waiting patiently for Michael to arrive.

He was right on time, and when I opened the door for him, I nearly fell backward. I really did not understand how a man could look that good every day of his life without even trying. He wore a pair of khaki cargo shorts and a plain white t-shirt with a pair of brown sandals. I was grinning like a school girl as he took my hand and led me to his pick-up truck. As soon as I fastened the seat belt and settled into my seat, Michael reached for my hand and grasped it as he put the truck in gear and backed out of his driveway. He held my hand throughout the entire drive.

We were both quiet as he drove into Hot Springs and navigated the streets of the small, bustling tourist town. His French singer's CD was playing on the car's stereo system. I had to admit that the crooner's voice was soothing as it poured from the speakers. Though I couldn't understand a single word, the groove of the music and the emotion behind the voice captured my attention and held it.

"What's this singer's name again?" I asked.

"Monsieur Nov," he said as he pulled into a parking lot.

"He is so good. I'm gonna have to get a copy of this CD."

He glanced at me. "You can have mine, if you want."

"Really?" I shook my head. "No, I'll get one."

"No, really. I want you to have it."

"Well, okay," I relented. "Thank you."

He parked the truck, rushed around to my side, and opened the passenger door for me. As I stepped out into the heat, I asked, "Where are we?"

"The airport."

"What? Why?"

"Like I said before, I wanna show you something."

My eyes were wide as we walked into the small terminal. I stood to the side while he spoke with the airport attendant, and then we were led out onto the tarmac to a small plane. When the attendant began to walk back to the terminal, I said, "What's going on?"

He smiled and swept his arm toward the plane. "We're going on a short flight."

I glanced up at the empty plane. "Who's gonna fly it?"

He chuckled. "I am."

"Huh... what?"

"*I am.*"

I scanned the tarmac, which was empty except for us and the plane that stood next to us. "Uh... you know how to fly a plane?"

"Um, yes... I do. They don't usually let you rent a plane without a license."

"How did you—you have a pilot's license?"

"Yeah, I underwent most of the training before you moved here, finished up the other day."

I glanced from his warm eyes to the plane and back. "Um... you just finished training?"

He rested his hand on my shoulder. "I've been licensed for years. I just underwent the training to upgrade my license, so that I can carry a passenger."

Well, that eased my mind… *a little*. "Uh…"

He stepped closer to me and wrapped his arms around my waist. "Do you think I would do anything that could possibly bring harm to you?" he asked softly.

I looked into his eyes, the eyes of a man who had saved my life and my heart, and I shook my head. "No, I don't."

He kissed my forehead. "Then, you trust me?"

I nodded. "I do."

He grinned as he released me. "Good."

He helped me into the front seat, closed the door, and climbed into the pilot's seat. I eyed the instruments as I buckled my seatbelt. My heart was beating about a thousand beats per minute. I trusted Michael, all right, but I was still scared. I'd heard too many stories about small planes crashing in the middle of nowhere. As Michael tinkered with the instruments, I uttered a silent prayer. I definitely wasn't ready to die.

The plane's engine started, and the propeller on the nose began to spin—slowly, then rapidly. I bit down on my bottom lip as the plane began to taxi on the runway, picking up more and more speed by the second. If I'd opted to eat a full breakfast rather than a bowl of cereal, I was sure that my entire stomach contents would have come rushing out of my mouth when Michael lifted the plane into the air.

As the plane ascended, I said another prayer.

"I think I'll always love the way this feels," Michael said, his eyes in front of him.

"W... what?" I asked as I tightly gripped my own thighs.

"Flying."

I squeezed my eyes shut as the plane continued to climb. "I thought you liked water," I said.

"I do. I like all of nature, including the sky."

"Well, I like the ground. The ground is really nice."

He chuckled. "The sky is better."

"If you say so."

As the plane leveled off, I opened my eyes to see that we were flying over Hot Springs. I could see the streets and houses below. I could see mountains in the distance. I could see the clouds as we passed them by. And I had to admit, the view was beautiful.

"Look," Michael said. "Look to the right."

I looked out the window and saw trees, lots of trees that looked like little green weeds beneath us. There was water—a lake. And small houses. Cabins.

"Is that Cook Lake?" I asked.

"Yes."

I smiled as I tried to make out which cabin was mine. "It looks beautiful from up here. *Everything* looks beautiful from up here."

"It sure does. God is awesome, Carla. *Awesome*."

"Yes, He truly is."

We flew for a while longer, over trees and lakes and mountains. Then he landed us safely at the airport. After we climbed back into his truck, I slid to the middle of the bench-like seat and kissed him on the cheek. "Thank you for today."

He looked into my eyes and smiled. "You're welcome. See what you miss when you stick to the ground? Sometimes, you gotta fly, Carla. Sometimes, you've just got to see things from a different vantage point in order to really appreciate them."

"You're right," I said, resting my head on his shoulder and closing my eyes as he drove us back to Cook Lake.

***

That night, we sat beneath the stars in Michael's back yard and talked. We talked about our jobs and our families and our feelings for each other—both of us agreeing that our attraction was strong, almost mystical in some ways. We held hands. We kissed. We held each other. What we had was pure on every level. There was no past between us to taint things. No motives or agendas. We were just two people who'd found each other and who needed each other. I believe we both went to Cook Lake looking for something in particular, not realizing that God had sent us there to find each other.

21

"The Way"

Over the next couple of weeks, we spent nearly every waking moment together, getting to know each other and just really enjoying each other's company. For the first time in a long time, I felt totally at ease and relaxed. In just a short while, Cook Lake and Michael Ross had changed my outlook on life and made me believe that my future could be a good one. My ex-husband hadn't crossed my mind in days, and some of the heaviness in my heart had lifted. My spirit felt lighter, but at the same time, I was gaining physical weight and was on my way back to my old, killer figure. But the amazing thing about Michael was that he liked me from the start, even when I was walking around looking like a female Skeletor.

I even stopped locking my door in the day time, and he stopped locking his. It was almost as if we both had two homes. We passed between our houses day in and day out. We ate all of our meals together. So when Michael walked into my cabin one Saturday morning with a grin on his face, I figured he was bringing me breakfast.

He walked into the kitchen and kissed me on the cheek. "Good morning, beautiful."

"Good morning, beautiful, yourself."

He laughed as he sat down across from me. "I don't think I've ever been called beautiful before."

"I don't know why not. You are certainly beautiful."

"Thank you. Um... have you eaten breakfast?"

I lifted my mug. "Not unless you consider coffee breakfast."

He shook his head. "You and your coffee. Well, let me see if I can do better than that." He stood from the table, opened the refrigerator, and began rummaging inside. He prepared an egg white omelet with spinach and cheese, wheat toast, and fruit. It was delicious and, of course, healthy. Afterwards, I showered and dressed, and Michael took me for a walk.

As we approached the woods, I expected us to take the same path we had before—the one that led to the lavender field. But instead, he bypassed that path and led me onto another path into the woods.

"Where are we going?" I asked.

"Um, I found something back here a few weeks ago that I—"

I stopped and held up a hand. "Let me guess, there's something you want to show me."

He laughed, and for some reason, I couldn't take my eyes off of his Adam's apple as it moved up and down. Something about that motion was just sexy to me. The man had the sexiest Adam's apple I'd ever seen in my life—and the sexiest neck and the sexiest skin, and—well, everything about him was very, *very* sexy. As he grabbed my hand and led me further into the woods, I shook my head a little, trying to shake off the lustful thoughts. And I was glad I did, because what he wanted to show me was a church. A very old, run-down, deserted church.

As we approached it, he released my hand and moved closer to the ramshackle building. "Look at it," he said with awe in his voice.

Okay, so maybe I was a little hardened from the things that had happened in my life, or maybe Michael was just a lunatic, because all I saw was a shack—the remnants of a structure that had long lost its luster. "Um… it looks like it used to be a church?" I said or asked or something.

He frowned slightly. "You don't see it?"

I stared at the building, at the glassless windows and the leaning walls. "See what?"

He dramatically opened his arms as if presenting something or someone to me. "The people streaming in and out of the doors, the people crowding the pews inside, the preacher wiping his brow as he delivers his sermon." He paused and moved closer to me, taking my hand and leading me to the doorway of the empty church. "The weddings, the christenings, the funerals. The lives that were lived and centered around this place. Can't you see it? Can't you *feel* it?"

I hesitantly shook my head and silently decided that one of us was definitely crazy, and it wasn't me. *I guess I always knew he was too good to be true*, I thought. *Oh, well.* "I don't see any of that, and it kind of concerns me that you *do*."

He shook his head. "You are thinking literally, I'm talking spiritually. I can see these things with my spiritual eyes. I can feel the life in this place. Will you do something for me?"

"What?" I asked.

"Close your eyes."

I frowned. "What?"

"Close your eyes. Close your eyes, and tell me what you see."

I sighed and then obliged him. I closed my eyes and stood still. After standing there for a full five minutes, I began to realize what he meant. No, I couldn't physically see anything, but I could imagine what he'd described, and the more I saw with my mind's eye, the more I felt the life of that place, the unique spirit that I'd once felt every time I stepped foot in a church. I'd missed that. I'd missed the spirit and love that flowed in that place—in my church. I'd missed the fellowship.

I opened my eyes and stepped into the empty church. I walked to where I imagined the altar once stood, and I kneeled before it. I lowered my head and dropped my eyes. This was hallowed ground—a place that deserved respect, *reverence*. I closed my eyes, and a few seconds later, I felt Michael kneel beside me and place his hand on my back. We stayed there, in that posture, for a long while—praying silently together. Then we stood to our feet and began making our way back home, hand-in-hand.

We had just approached the tree line when he stopped short of stepping onto the road. He turned and looked at me. "There's something I need to tell you," he said softly. There was worry in his eyes, tension in his voice.

"What... what is it?"

He sighed as he dropped my hand and backed up against a tree. He smoothed a tuft of hair behind his ear and closed his eyes. "I haven't told you the whole truth about some things."

My heart jumped into my throat. *Oh, hell.* "Like what? Are you... are you *gay*?" *Please, God. Don't let that be it. I don't think I could take that again.*

He opened his eyes and grinned slightly. "No, Carla. I'm not gay."

"Bi?"

He shook his head. "No."

I felt a little relieved. "Then what is it?"

A somber expression clouded his face. "I haven't been 100% truthful about how my wife died."

"You... you said she was sick, that she was sick when you met her." *Oh, Lord, please don't tell me you killed her.*

"She *was*, but there's something specific about her illness that I need to tell you."

I just stood there and stared at him. I wasn't sure how to feel or what to say, and I was too afraid of what he might say next to speak anyway.

"She died from complications of AIDS. She was HIV positive when I met her."

I backed into a tree and tried to calm my heart and catch my breath at the same time. "What? Did you know? I mean..."

"She told me when we first met. I fell in love with her anyway. It didn't matter to me."

Despite the summer heat enveloping me, I hugged my body. "Um, Michael... are you, uh..."

He waved his hands in front of him. "No, I'm not HIV positive, and I have the test results to prove it."

"Oh, uh... okay. How did she... um..."

"She was raped when she was fairly young. She lived with HIV for years, thought she'd never get married. She said men would run away from her when she told them."

I looked into his eyes—his warm, beautiful eyes. "But you didn't run."

"No, I didn't." He hesitated. "I... um, I wanted to ask you, Carla. Have you been tested?"

I frowned. "Tested?"

He nodded. "Were you tested for STDs at the hospital—when you were treated for the miscarriage?"

I shifted my eyes to the ground. "I don't know. I mean, I'm not sure."

"You should check on that. You never know. If it was possible for you to get pregnant and he had been cheating like you said, you really should get checked out."

I nodded. This was something I hadn't been ready to face. At that moment, I still wasn't ready.

He took my hand in his and began to lead me back to our cabins. "No matter the results, I'll be here for you," he said as he slipped his arm around my waist.

And I had no doubt that he was telling the truth.

We went straight to his cabin, where he showed me his test results—three years of negative test results. I breathed a little easier after seeing them. But questions about my own status were stuck in the back of my mind as we ate lunch together. So, after lunch, I decided to go back to my place for a little alone time, so that I could wrap my mind around what he'd told me about his wife and about myself. I'd left my phone at my place and upon my return, found that I had missed a couple of calls from my mother. She didn't leave any messages, so I decided to call her back in the morning.

I spent the remainder of the day alone with my thoughts and internal questions, but there were three things I knew for certain—that I loved Michael even more after learning the truth about his late wife, that he was truly a good man, and that he was right about me needing to be tested.

***

The next morning, I went to Michael's cabin and took my turn cooking us breakfast. Afterwards, we were snuggling up on the floor in front of his couch, enjoying our coffee and each other's company, when my phone began to buzz and dance across his coffee table. Michael leaned over and kissed me. "Leave it," he whispered against my lips.

"Unh-uh. It could be one of my sons."

He relented and backed away from me a little. I grabbed the phone and frowned. The call was from my mother. "Hello? Mama?" I answered.

"Carla Sue, I've been trying to call you. Mrs. Tooley took a turn for the worse yesterday afternoon. We rushed her to the hospital, but it was too late, sweetie. We need you to come home, baby. She passed on a few minutes ago. Your daddy just broke down."

My hand flew to my mouth. "Oh, Mama! Okay, I'm on my way now."

"Be careful."

"I will."

I hung up and looked at Michael, who wore a concerned expression on his face. "What is it?" he asked.

"My grandmother died. I need to go be with my family."

"I'm so sorry to hear that. Give me a minute, and I'll be ready to go."

I grabbed his arm. "Wait, where are you going?"

"With you," he said matter-of-factly.

"No, that's not necessary, I—"

"I'm not letting you go back to that town, where your ex-husband lives, *alone*. I'll drop you off at your parents' house and pick you up when you're ready to come back."

"Michael—"

"I'm not taking no for an answer."

I sighed. "Fine, but we're taking my vehicle. I doubt if yours will make it."

He raised an eyebrow and hopped to his feet, then offered me his hand and helped me up from the floor. "What makes you say that? You've ridden in my truck before. It runs like a dream."

"I've ridden in it for short distances."

"My truck could outrun yours any day."

"I don't know... I'm just saying, is it safe? I mean, it's a long way to Pine Bluff."

He grasped my hand and planted a kiss on my cheek before walking me to his door. "See you in a few minutes. You'll see what the old girl can do."

I sighed. There was obviously no changing his mind. "Okay," I said softly.

He held my face in his hands. "Hey, you gonna be okay?"

I looked up at him and nodded. "Yeah, I just need to get home. I'm worried about my father."

He pulled me into a hug and said, "I'll have you there in no time."

22

"Them Changes"

I wasn't overwhelmingly sad about my grandmother's death. I felt the loss, of course, and a little nostalgia as my mind quickly drifted back to the good times—the times my brother and I would visit her riverside home as children and help her tend her garden and clean the fish she'd catch. But I wasn't especially down about her passing. She'd lived a long life, and her mind was almost completely gone by the end. When she was younger, she always expressed that she never wanted to be a burden to anyone. If she'd been cognizant of her condition, it would've really upset her. I saw her death as a healing. In Heaven, she wouldn't have dementia anymore.

I also knew that though my mother was the sweetest woman in the world, she had to be tired. Taking care of my grandmother was like taking care of a baby who took tons of pills and insulin injections, only there were times when this baby would remember how to walk and run the risk of falling and hurting herself. Mama would never admit it, but I was sure she was weary. For her, I was relieved.

It was my father that I was concerned about. My heart broke for him. Of Mamie Tooley's six children, my father was the youngest and the only son. His father had died when he was twelve, and from that point on, he'd been the man of the house. He was very close to his mother. I knew he was deeply hurt by her passing.

I glanced over at Michael in the driver's seat of his truck. The truck actually made for a smooth ride, and I really didn't know why I thought it wouldn't since I'd ridden in it before. During the ride, my mind was occupied with all of the tasks ahead of me. I would have to help with the planning of the services and offer as much support as I could to my father. I'd also have to call Bryan and ask him to bring the boys to the funeral. I dreaded that more than I did the thought of my father having to bury his beloved mother.

I glanced over at Michael again. His eyes were fixed on the windshield. "You're right. This truck actually rides smoothly," I said.

He winked and nodded his head. "I know. How're you holding up over there?"

"I'm okay. Just worried about my dad. I'll be glad when we get there."

"Yeah. I know how he feels. I lost both of my parents a few years back. They died less than a year apart. It was really hard on me."

"I'm so sorry. You've been through so much, but you still seem so happy."

"I *am* happy. God keeps sending me blessings. I mean, just look at you. *Look at you.* How can I not be happy?" He reached over and squeezed my hand.

I felt a warmth travel through my entire body. "Thank you for driving me, Michael."

"Of course. I'm gonna pick you up when you're ready to come back to the lake. You *are* coming back, right?"

I smiled at him. "Of course I am. I'll miss you."

"I already miss you," he said softly.

I leaned over, kissed his cheek, and rested my head on the back of the seat as I gazed out the window. Before I knew it, the ride had lulled me to sleep.

***

After a week of bunking with my parents, planning the funeral, and waiting for out-of-town relatives to arrive, I attended my grandmother's home-going celebration on a sunny Saturday afternoon in the church to which I belonged but hadn't stepped foot in since, well, since my world exploded. The sanctuary was packed with extended family members, family friends, and church members. Bryan had dropped the boys off at my parents' house all dressed in their Sunday best. I was glad to have them there sitting beside me. I'd missed them more than I realized. Marli and her husband were also there to support me, and just before service began, a vision walked into the sanctuary and garnered the attention of nearly everyone in attendance. I'd given him the details regarding the funeral when we spoke on the phone the night before, but I didn't expect him to come. Then again, it was so like him to show up and offer his support.

Michael stood out not only as the only non-black in the room, but also because of his spirit and his beauty. I knew I loved him before that moment, but right at that second, I knew I would *always* love him. I caught his eye as he took a seat at the back of the church. I smiled at him, and he nodded at me. I suddenly wished we were married so that he could sit with me in the family section. Then I decided that he *was* family. He was in my heart, and that was as close as a person could get to being family. So I stood and scooted past my family members on the pew and walked to the back of the church. I reached for his hand, and with an uncertain look on his face, he followed me back to my seat and held my hand throughout the service. We received some strange looks, but I didn't care. He was there to support me, and I needed his support.

After the interment, I invited Michael to my parents' house where I introduced him to much of the crowd crammed inside. I was in the middle of introducing him to some of my cousins when Marli grabbed my arm and pulled me aside.

"Girl, you didn't describe him adequately. Good grief! He is *gorgeous*!!" she gushed.

"I *did* try to tell you, but you wouldn't listen."

"Well, I'm sorry. He is *beautiful* and those shoulders? Wow! He's so regal, like he actually descended from a king or an Indian chief or something. How tall is he? He's even taller than Chris! Shoot, he looks taller than Bryan."

"I don't know, I think he's around 6'6". And his body? Girl, he looks absolutely irresistible naked."

Her eyes widened. "Wait, you've seen him naked?!"

"Shh!" I hissed. "It's not what you think. Remember the skinny dipping I told you about?" I lowered my voice. "Marli, I feel like a girl again. How can it be possible to feel so... so connected to someone I barely know? I really think I'm in love with him, but that is just insane!"

"That's not insane. I can see why you would feel that way. There is just something about him…"

"You don't think I'm crazy? I've only known him for a few weeks."

"I'm married to a white man with a black family, and my kids are eighteen years apart. Who am I to call you crazy?"

"I just hope I'm not making a mistake with him. I mean... I really, *really* want to be with him, but I think I should slow down, but I can't slow down," I rambled.

Marli chuckled. "Yeah, you're in love."

I laughed, too. Then I remembered I was at a funeral gathering and stopped myself. "Girl, I think I want to have this man's babies, and I'm really too old to be thinking like that."

"Dang, *really*? Things are that serious? Um, Carla, I need to ask you something, but I'm only asking you this because you asked me the same thing once. I figure turnabout is fair play."

I frowned slightly. "What is it?"

She lowered her voice to a conspiratorial tone. "Um, is he any good?"

I backed away from her a little and shrugged. "I wouldn't know, Marli. We haven't done it."

"What?!" she shrieked softly and then stood there with her mouth hung open and her eyes bugged to capacity.

"Wow, Marli. Really? You gotta react like that? I just buried my grandmother, and you're up in here acting up."

She shrugged. "God rest Grandma Tooley's soul, but I'm just saying..."

"Whatever."

"Excuse me, sister. I just wanted to be sure to give you my condolences." It was Shauna Parker, *Deacon Lamar Parker's wife*, who'd interrupted us. She was visibly pregnant with a small child in tow and a sorrowful look on her face.

"I only met Mrs. Tooley once, I believe, but her spirit was so beautiful," she continued. "I just wanted you to know that I'm praying for your family."

I glanced at Marli, then turned my attention back to the young woman who, along with her husband, was at least ten years younger than me and Bryan. "Um... thank you," I said.

"It's good to see you again, sister," she said with a soft smile.

"Yes. Same here."

"Okay, well, I better be going. My husband's home sick. He's sorry he couldn't make it."

My stomach lurched. "Okay. Um... thanks for coming."

As soon as she was out of earshot, I said, "I need to get out of here and get back to your cabin. That was just too much for me."

"What?" Marli asked, sounding and looking confused.

I steered her outside onto the front lawn. "That was my husband's lover's wife. Poor thing's pregnant again, and he's still sneaking around with Bryan."

Marli gasped. "That was her? I wonder if she knows."

"She *can't* know." I shook my head. "Someone should tell her."

"Who, besides you?"

"No, unh-uh, it can't be me."

"Then who? The woman needs to know. Wouldn't you want to know?"

"I *do* know. That's the problem."

"Do you think you would've been better off not knowing?"

I sighed. "No. It was best that I found out. I just don't want to be the one to tell her, but I know I'm the only one who *can*. I could kill Bryan for putting me in this position."

"Hmm," Marli said. "Look who you spoke up."

I rolled my eyes as I watched Bryan park his vehicle on the street in front of my parents' house. We watched as he made his way up the front sidewalk to where we stood on the lawn.

"Hey, Marli. Man, you're looking good," he said.

"Bryan," Marli said with a slight nod and more than a slight amount of irritation in her voice.

"Um, hey, Carla. Can I speak to you for a moment?" he asked.

Marli frowned and placed her hand on my arm. I turned and gave her a nod. "It's okay."

She slowly walked back into the house, and I turned my attention to Bryan. "Yes?"

"I was at the funeral," he informed me.

I shrugged. "I didn't see you. Thanks for coming."

"I saw you."

"Okay…"

"You messing around with that Indian you were sitting with?"

I tilted my head to the side. "Why? You like him? You wanna mess around with him? Fine, ain't he? But, oops. He ain't gay.

Better luck next time."

"You always did have a mouth on you. You better watch how you talk to me."

"Or what? If there's one place where I know I'm safe, it's here with my daddy and his shot gun, not to mention my brother and cousins who are only a few feet away. You even put your pinky finger on me, and it'll be the last thing you do, and you know it."

"I don't like the looks of him. I don't want him around my sons."

"Are you serious right now? You lost the right to make those kinds of demands when you decided to cheat on me in the same house with YOUR sons. Your child even saw the man leave. You cannot be serious right now."

"I made a mistake. That doesn't give you the right—" he stopped mid-sentence. His eyes were fixed on my parents' porch. I followed his gaze to see Michael standing there with his arms folded across his chest. His eyes were focused on Bryan, and there was not even the hint of a smile on his face. He looked intimidating to say the least. If I didn't know for myself that he was a gentle soul, *I* would've been scared of him.

Bryan backed away from me a little, glanced at Michael, and said, "You can drop the boys off at my mom's later."

I watched him leave and was about to join Michael on the porch when I felt a hand on my shoulder. He'd joined me on the front lawn.

"Are you okay?" he asked.

I smiled up at him. "I'm fine. Are you having fun meeting my family?"

He chuckled. "Actually, I am. One of your aunts asked me what reservation I live on. Your cousin, Inez, slipped me her phone number, and one of your nephews asked me what my real name is, because, as he put it, Michael Ross is not an Indian name."

I covered my face with my hands. "Oh, Lord, I'm sorry."

He shrugged and wrapped his arm around my shoulder. "It's not the first time I've heard any of those questions, and it won't be the last."

I leaned into him and sighed. "Thanks again for coming. It really means a lot to me."

"I'm glad to be here. Glad I got to meet your family, especially your boys."

"Yeah, they like you. They think you're cool."

He kissed my forehead. "I like them, too. Your mom offered to let me spend the night here tonight. I told her I could get a hotel room."

"But she insisted, right?"

"Right."

"Well, it'll be good having you here. You can get to know my folks a little better, and we can head out in the morning as planned."

"As long as I get to take you back to the lake, I'm happy."

I hugged him and rested my head on his chest. "I can't wait."

"Hmm."

"Hey, I need to make a stop in the morning before we head back."

"Okay. Whatever you want."

***

We had a great time with my family that night, despite the somber occasion for which we were gathered. My parents and my brother, Walter, had a ball telling Michael all about my childhood, making sure to emphasize the more embarrassing low points—me wetting the bed during a sleepover when I was eleven, my first car wreck at fifteen, and on and on. Michael shared his childhood with us, including some of the Cherokee folklore he'd learned from his father. My boys hung on his every word and were disappointed when Michael and I took them to their other grandmother's house.

When Michael and I separated to go to bed that night, my thoughts were of him and how well he got along with my family. My mind was full of possibilities for us. Possibilities of a future together. But as I drifted off to sleep, my mind shifted to the task at hand for the next morning—my conversation with Shauna Parker.

23

"Blame It on Me"

I got the Parkers' number from my father, who was also a deacon at our church. I told him I just wanted to call and thank Mrs. Parker for the cake she'd made for the repass. I hated to lie to him, but I just didn't have the heart to tell him the truth, partially because I didn't want to have to say the words more than once in the same day. I called her early that morning and made light conversation, hoping that she would indicate whether or not her husband was home. She did.

"I hope I'm not bothering you or your husband by calling so early, but I'm heading out of town in a little while."

"Oh, no, it's just me and the kids. Lamar is at work."

I looked over at Michael, who was sitting in the driver's seat of his truck hanging on my every word. "Oh, well, would it be okay for me to drop by for a few minutes on my way out?"

"Oh..." I could hear the curiosity and uncertainty in her voice, but just like any other good church member, she said, "Well, sure. Do you know the address?"

"Yes," I said.

About fifteen minutes later, Michael pulled into the Parkers' driveway and turned his truck off. "You want me to go in with you?"

I shook my head. "This is going to be hard enough for her. I don't think she needs an audience."

He nodded, leaned over, and softly kissed my cheek. Then he squeezed my hand. "I'll be right here."

I gave him a nervous smile as I climbed out of the truck and stepped onto the bleached, white driveway. I slowly made my way to the front door of the beautiful two-story home that reminded me so much of my old home with Bryan—my dream home. I wondered if this was Shauna Parker's dream home. I wondered if she would ever recover from what I was about to tell her.

I rang the shiny, new doorbell and held my breath. Under a minute later, Mrs. Parker graced the doorway wearing a pair of jeans and an oversized church anniversary t-shirt. *Probably her husband's shirt,* I thought. She gave me a nervous, unconvincing smile. I returned hers with a regretful smile of my own.

"Come in," she said as she cleared the doorway for me. "Would you like some water, or maybe some juice?" she asked as she led me through the spotless foyer into a beautifully, if slightly overly, decorated living room.

I took a seat on the sofa and said, "No, thank you."

She sat across from me in a recliner and began rocking back and forth. "Well, I was a little surprised when you asked to come over. I assume it's about your grandmother or the funeral? I really am sorry about her passing. She was a sweetheart."

I clasped my hands in my lap and inspected my chipped nail polish before lifting my head to face the pretty young woman with the fragile-looking, small frame and swollen belly. "Thank you, but no, that's not why I'm here."

"Oh..."

"I'm sure you've heard about my divorce. I know it has to be the talk of the church."

She frowned slightly. "Well, yes. I... I heard about that."

"We'd been separated for a few years before our divorce was finalized. We were both unfaithful, but Bryan was unfaithful first, and I-uh... never got over it."

"Why are you telling me this?"

I cleared my throat and avoided her eyes. "Because something happened during our marriage that involves *your* marriage. I'm really sorry to have to tell you this, but I believe you have a right to know, and—"

She let out a harsh breath and sprang up from her seat. "It... it's *you*. You're the one he keeps sneaking out of the house to be with! I *knew* he was cheating. It's you!"

I stood from the sofa and raised my hands. "No, no, it's not—"

"What did you hope to accomplish by coming here and telling me this? He's not gonna leave me. He *can't* leave me! He can't afford the child support!"

"No, listen—"

"No, *you* listen! You might have ruined your own marriage, but I'm not gonna let you ruin mine. He is mine, you hear me? And I'm not giving him away to you or none of these other sluts around here!"

"I didn't have an affair with him! My husband did!" I blurted. So much for the soft approach, but she'd left me no other choice.

She stood there and stared at me, her mouth hung open, her hand resting on her stomach. Then she eased herself back down onto the recliner. "You're lying," she said softly.

"I wish I was."

A child peeped around the corner. "Go back to your room, Junior," Shauna Parker said, fixing her eyes on the floor.

We sat there in silence for a few seconds, then she looked up at me and said, "How do I know you're not lying?"

"My marriage is over. *Look at me.* Do I look like I'm lying?"

She sighed deeply. "How? When?"

"I caught them in my own bed together four years ago."

"Four years ago? And you're telling me now? Maybe... maybe it was just a one-time thing—"

I shook my head. "That's what Bryan told me—that they were just experimenting, that it would never happen again. But then I caught them together again, meeting at Bryan's office, and... and I saw them together at a motel recently. I have a picture."

She stared at me as I scrolled to the picture of Bryan and Lamar hugging and held my phone up for her to see. Her eyes widened as she stood and rushed out of the room. I followed her into the kitchen, where she was hunched over the garbage can, heaving.

I rested my hand on her back. "Is there anything I can do to help you?"

She shook her head as she wiped her mouth. "You can leave."

"I'm sorry—"

She looked up at me with red eyes; her pale, brown skin was flushed. "Get out!"

I held up my hands and backed away from her. "Okay." As I turned to leave, I said, "I really am sorry."

I quickly left the house, feeling like I was fleeing the scene of a heinous crime. I guess a crime had been committed, though. It just wasn't my crime, or was it?

As I climbed into the truck, Michael said, "You okay?"

I shook my head and buried my face in my hands. "No, I just ruined that woman's life."

He reached over and rested his hand on my arm. "No, you didn't. This is not your fault."

I sighed. "Then why do I feel so bad about it?"

"Because you know exactly what she's going through."

I stared at the house as he backed out of the driveway. "What do I do now?"

"Pray. That's all anyone can do."

***

Being back at the lake felt more like being at home to me than when I was actually back in Pine Bluff. I'd missed the tranquility and peace that I'd only known at Cook Lake, and I'd missed being alone with Michael.

As I sat beside him at the end of the pier with my feet dangling over the water, I tried to clear my mind of an image that had haunted me since I left Pine Bluff. I tried to erase the horrified look that the young Mrs. Parker had worn when I showed her the picture of our husbands locked in an embrace. I sighed as I stared across the lake at the lights filling the windows of the other cabins.

"Are you all right?" Michael asked.

I shrugged. "As all right as I can be."

"Thinking about the funeral?"

"You'd think so, but, no. My mind was on something else."

"Your conversation with the young lady?"

I nodded. "I feel horrible for being the one to have to break it to her. I know how she feels. She feels like the rug has been pulled out from under her—like everything she thought was real and true was really just an illusion."

"Do you still feel like that?" he asked.

I stared at him in the moonlight and wondered why that question seemed so difficult for me to answer. "I did at first, but now... I don't know."

He reached for my hand. "It's okay if you still have hurt feelings about what happened between you and your ex-husband. It's normal. Do you still love him?"

I shook my head. "No."

With raised eyebrows, he said, "Are you sure?"

"Positive."

"Are you still afraid of him?"

I frowned. "I wasn't the day of the funeral. But I think he's afraid of *you*."

"He should be. He thinks you're his property. He's wrong."

I gave him a wry grin. "Whose property am I, then? Yours?"

"No. God's and only God's."

I nodded and refocused my attention on our across-the-lake neighbors.

"Your family is funny," he said with a chuckle.

I smiled, glad he'd changed the subject. "I know. I'm so sorry. I cannot believe they said all of that stuff to you."

"Yeah, I was okay until your brother asked me if I lived in a tepee."

I shook my head. "I'm so ashamed of him. He is an educated man. He knew better than that!"

"And then your aunt asked me about my name, too, said Michael Ross couldn't possibly be my name. She asked me what my 'Injun' name was. Your family was really obsessed with my name."

"Oh, Dear Lord. I am so sorry, Michael. I really am. I don't think anyone in my family has ever met a Native American before, but that's no excuse for them asking that stuff."

"Atsadi," he said.

"What?"

"My Cherokee name is Atsadi."

"Oh…"

"You didn't ask, but you wanted to."

"I actually hadn't even thought about it."

"Mm-hmm."

"Whatever. What does the name mean?"

"Fish. My father gave me that name, because he said that even as an infant, I loved water."

"Atsadi. I like it. What name would you give me?"

"Hmmm, a Cherokee name for you? How about Awenasa? Yes, I think that fits."

"What's it mean?"

"She who asks too many questions."

I splashed some water on him with my foot. "Whatever! What does it really mean?"

He smiled as he leaned in close to me and softly kissed my lips. "Maybe I'll tell you one day."

"Trying to be all mysterious, huh?"

He stared at me for a moment, took me into his arms, and laid a kiss on me that made me forget my next thought.

***

The first thing that woke me up the next morning was the ringing of my cell phone, which was closely followed by knocks at my back door. I grabbed my phone and stumbled to the back door to open it as I answered the call. At the door was Michael, who still knocked sometimes, though I never locked the door. He walked into my kitchen and lightly kissed my cheek as I placed my phone to my ear and said, "Hello?"

"What the hell is wrong with you?!" Bryan blasted in my ear.

I pulled the phone from my ear and frowned. What the hell was his problem? I activated the speaker phone and laid the phone on the table as I sat down across from Michael. "Bryan, it's too early in the morning for this. What are you talking about?"

"I did everything you asked! I went along with everything you wanted in the divorce!"

I sighed. "Uh... yeah, you did. Because you had no choice. Do we really need to rehash this right now? I haven't even had my coffee yet."

"Why did you show that picture to Lamar's wife?"

I cringed at hearing him say his lover's name. "Because she deserved to know, and evidently, Lamar isn't man enough to tell her."

"It was not your business to tell her anything! She's put him out of the house. You have ruined their marriage. Are you happy now?!"

"No, Bryan. *You* ruined his marriage. You and Lamar. The two of you ruined *both* of our marriages."

"If I knew where you were right now, I'd beat the hell out of you right where you stand!"

"Oh, there he is! The *real* Slim Shady Foster!"

"Hang up," Michael said in an even, but stern, voice.

Before I could reply to either of them, Bryan said, "Who the hell is that?! Is that that Indian? You shacking up with that Indian, Carla?! Tell him I'll beat him down, too."

"I doubt that, friend, but you can try," Michael said. Then he ended the call.

"Hey!" I shouted at Michael. "Why'd you do that?! Why'd you hang up?!"

"Because you *wouldn't* hang up. It made no sense for you to keep talking to him. Nothing was gonna come of that conversation. At least nothing constructive."

"He has my sons, Michael. What if he needed to tell me something about them?"

"I would think that would've been the first thing he mentioned. And besides, I've met your boys. They're not babies. If they need to talk to you or to tell you something, they can call you themselves."

I shook my head. "You don't have kids. You wouldn't understand."

"I understand that you *wanted* to argue with him. I think you enjoy it."

"Enjoy it? Are you serious? He *raped* me, Michael. I don't enjoy talking to him at all, *ever!* I wish he'd just disappear from the face of the earth!"

"Could've fooled me."

"What is that supposed to mean?!"

Before he could answer me, my phone began to ring again, and Bryan's name flashed across the screen.

Michael lifted his eyes from the phone and stared at me. I stared right back at him, and in the middle of our little stare-off, the phone quit ringing only to start right back up again. This time, I picked it up and answered it, my eyes glued to Michael. There was one thing he was going to have to figure out quickly: no one runs me.

"Hello!" I barked into the phone.

Michael shook his head, stood from the table, and left my cabin, slamming the back door behind him. For the next twenty minutes, I argued senselessly with Bryan, and when I finally hung up, I felt like a fool.

24

"Knockin'"

I spent the rest of that day holed up inside of my cabin. Michael never came back to my door, and I never went to his. And… I missed him. He was right, and I knew it. I *had* wanted to talk to Bryan—to argue with him. I wanted to say mean things to him and to sling sexually oriented slurs at him. I wanted to damn him to hell. I actually felt joy when I did those things to him, and that was wrong. I knew that. In my mind, I was sure that those were the wrong things to do. But in my heart? That was a different story. He'd hurt my heart, damaged it nearly beyond repair. When I said those things to him, my heart felt a little better. But it never felt as good as it did when I was with Michael Ross.

The next morning, I swallowed my pride, hung my head, and walked over to his cabin to apologize. I knocked on his back door for several minutes, but received no answer. I stood there and wondered if he was so mad at me that he was ignoring my knocks. I knew he was home, because his truck was parked in front of the cabin, and I'd been watching his place all morning. If he'd left on foot, I would've seen him. Then a flood of scenarios crowded my mind. *What if he had another woman in there? What if he had a man in there? What if he was dead or hurt or something?*

I shook my head. *You are really losing it*, I thought. I knocked again and tried the knob. It was locked, of course. I sighed and turned to head back to my cabin and then decided to check the front of his cabin. It was so quiet that morning, quieter than any other morning in a long time. There were no birds chirping, no bugs making noises. The air was thick and dry and hot. There was no wind, and everything was eerily still. The hairs on my arms stood at attention. I rubbed my arms and knocked on the front door. No answer. I knocked again and again—still no answer. At that point, I was almost sure that something was wrong. He was in there. I *knew* he was. And even if he was mad at me, he wouldn't just ignore me like that. That wasn't in his nature as far as I could tell.

I grasped the doorknob, turned it, and opened the door. I was so surprised that it was unlocked; I quickly shut it back. Then I slowly opened it again, peeked my head inside, and shouted, "Michael! Are you home?"

I strained my ears for a full minute. Nothing.

"Michael! Um, it's Carla."

Nothing, then… *something*. A sound, a gurgle or a moan. I wasn't sure, but I knew it had come from a human being.

I opened the door enough to ease my body inside. Then I shut it and stood in the living room, where there was no sign of him. I walked slowly through the living room to the kitchen—no Michael. I made my way down the dark hallway to the guest bedroom—he wasn't there, either. I walked into the master bedroom to see that he hadn't made his bed. His running clothes were laid across a chair in the corner of the room. I scanned the room and saw something that nearly made me scream—a pair of feet, *Michael's* feet. He was lying on the floor, in the bathroom doorway. Most of his body was lying on the bathroom floor, but he was so tall that his legs and feet were on the bedroom floor. I rushed to him and found him lying on his back with his eyes open, but they weren't focused on anything. When I said his name, his eyes didn't focus on me. I fell to the floor beside him and placed a trembling hand on the cold, clammy skin of his forehead. His breathing was shallow. I wanted to panic, but I told myself that I was a healthcare professional. I was trained to deal with things like this. *Think, think!* I told myself.

I scanned the floor around him, and that's when I saw it—a blood glucose monitor, along with several test strips and lancets that were scattered near him. I frowned as I picked the monitor up and then looked back down at Michael. Had he been in the middle of checking his blood sugar when whatever happened, happened? Was he diabetic? I quickly placed the strip in the machine, pricked his finger, and watched as the blood was sucked into the strip. Seconds later, his blood sugar registered on the screen—*55*. His blood sugar was low—*dangerously* low.

I sprang to my feet and rushed to the kitchen. I needed to get some sugar into him *fast*. I spotted some packets of sugar on the table and thought about something I'd seen a nurse do once before. I rushed back to his side, opened his mouth, and lifted his tongue. Then I opened a packet of sugar and poured it under his tongue. I waited a few seconds before opening another packet and pouring it into his mouth, too. In less than a minute, he was becoming more alert. He blinked a few times, coughed a little, and smiled up at me. "Hey, beautiful," he whispered.

I returned his smile, collapsed onto his chest, and wrapped my arms around him. "You're okay. You're okay…"

***

"Why didn't you tell me you were diabetic?" I asked as I sat across the table from Michael, watching him eat the breakfast I'd just cooked for him.

He shrugged. "Because, of all of the millions of questions you've asked me, that wasn't one of them, and besides, I didn't think it was important. I've been seeing my doctor pretty regularly. I thought things were under control."

"Well, it *is* important. You scared me. I mean, you *really* scared me."

"Didn't mean to. Thanks for saving me. What were you doing over here so early anyway?"

I wrapped my hand around my coffee mug and sighed. "I wanted to apologize for yesterday. I was acting a fool, and I'm sorry. You were right. It didn't make any sense for me to sit there and argue with Bryan."

"It's okay. I'm just glad you figured things out so you could come over here and save my life."

"How long have you been diabetic?"

"Since I was a kid."

I frowned and leaned forward. "Then how in the world did you let your sugar get that low? You should know better!"

"You upset me, and I forgot to eat dinner."

I raised an eyebrow and leaned back a little. "So this is *my* fault?"

He shook his head. "I didn't say that. I'm just telling the truth. I was upset because we fought, and I didn't eat."

"Well, I'm sorry. I guess I'll have to make it up to you." I stood and walked around to his side of the table. He smiled up at me as I slid into his lap. "You know what we haven't done yet?"

His eyes were focused on my neck as I wrapped my arms around him. "Uh... I can think of a couple of things we haven't done yet."

I rubbed my hand over his hair. "Not *those* things."

"What then?"

"We've never been out on a real date. You've never even seen me with make-up on or with my hair done up."

"You're beautiful just the way you are. I don't need to see that."

"I've never seen you dressed up, either. Although I don't see how you could possibly look any better than you do right now."

He squeezed me and rested his head on my chest. "You think I look good?"

"You know I do."

He reached up and softly kissed me. "Thank you."

Before I could reply, my cell phone began to ring and vibrate against his kitchen table. It was Bryan. I hesitated to answer it. As a matter of fact, I didn't move a muscle. I didn't want to argue with Michael again, but there was the thought in the back of my mind that it could be about my boys.

"Answer it," Michael said, releasing his hold on me.

I looked from the phone to his face. "If it's not about the boys, I'm hanging up."

He nodded and pushed his chair back a little. I reached over to the phone and pressed the button to answer the call. Then I put it on speakerphone. "Hello?" I said.

"Hey, it's me. I need to talk to you about something." Bryan sounded calm, almost dignified. But I couldn't trust that.

"Is it about the boys?" I asked.

"Huh? Um, no, it's not about the boys, It's about something I got in the mail today. Were you—"

"If it's not about the boys, we have nothing to talk about."

"Carla—"

I ended the call before he could finish his statement. Of course he called right back, and I ignored the call.

"That was kinda rude, you know?" Michael said with a slight grin on his face.

"But you enjoyed it, didn't you?"

"Yeah. He deserved it. He deserves worse for violating you and threatening to do it again. What kind of man does stuff like that?"

I shrugged. "Spoiled, mama's boy dentists, I guess. Bryan's used to getting his way. He never could control me, but he *had* me. I was his. He just can't seem to get over the fact that I'm not anymore. He doesn't understand why I couldn't just let what happened be in the past and give him another chance. What he fails to realize is that I *did* give him another chance, and he blew it."

"And he got so angry that he raped you?"

"Yeah. I really didn't see that coming. He was never violent toward me before. *Never.*"

He wrapped his arms around me again. "I'm sorry."

"Me, too."

He leaned in and kissed me. I was in the middle of returning the kiss when my phone rang again. I groaned against Michael's lips.

"Him, again?" he asked.

I glanced at the phone. "No, it's my mom."

I answered the phone, placing it to my ear as Michael lightly kissed my neck. "Hello? Mama?"

"Hey, baby. How are you this morning?" she replied.

I dug my fingers into Michael's hair as he hugged me tighter and kissed my cheek. "I'm fine. Is everything okay?"

"Yes, me and your daddy are fine. Um, I do need to ask you about something, though."

"Okay…"

"I love you," Michael whispered into my ear.

"I love you, too," I mouthed.

"Did you talk to Shauna Parker when you were home for the funeral? I know you got her number from your daddy," Mama said.

I stood from Michael's lap and reclaimed my chair at the table so that I could focus on what Mama was saying. "Um, yes, ma'am. Why?"

"What did you talk to her about?" she asked, ignoring my question.

"Mama, what's going on?"

She sighed. "Well, the talk around town is that she beat the mess out of her husband with an iron. The man's got a black eye and bruises everywhere. They say she put him out, too. I was wondering if whatever you discussed with her had anything to do with it."

"Yeah, I'm sure it did."

Silence from both of us.

"You're not going to tell me what's going on, huh?" she asked.

"I would, but I really don't want to say it out loud. Not now. Not today."

"Hmm, one day?"

"Yes, ma'am. One day. Anyway, how is it that you don't know? Usually, you know everything before it happens."

"I know what the dreams tell me—my dreams, other folks' dreams. Haven't been no dreams about Shauna Parker beating the living daylights out of her husband."

"Well, then, maybe God is protecting you because, believe me, you really don't wanna know."

"You know, you might be right, because it seems like whatever is going on is a mess and a half."

"It's two or three messes."

"Well, I'll let you go. Tell Michael I said hi. I know he's probably sitting there staring at you."

I glanced over at Michael, who was doing just what she said. I smiled. "Why would he be doing that?"

"Because I don't need a dream to tell me that man is crazy about you. I saw that when he was here. And you're crazy about him, too."

"Bye, Mama."

"You don't have to admit it for it to be the truth. Bye, Carla Sue."

I hung up and shook my head.

"What?" Michael asked.

"She thinks you're crazy about me."

"I am."

I was grinning and blushing so hard at that point, I was sure I looked stupid. "Thank you. She also said that I'm crazy about you."

With raised eyebrows, he asked, "Are you?"

"I have been since the moment I laid eyes on you," I admitted.

"Then why did you push me away?"

I dropped my eyes, feeling a little weird about my feelings and having to share them with him. "I wasn't sure if you liked me like that, and I thought you weren't over your wife's passing, and I was… uh, I was kind of afraid of you, or at least I was afraid of the way you made me feel."

He stood from his chair and reached for my hand, pulling me to my feet. As he drew me into his arms, he said, "How did I make you feel?"

I placed my hands on his wide chest and looked up at him. "Like I could fall in love with you. I didn't ever want to fall in love again."

He smiled as he leaned in and kissed me for a long, lingering moment. "Glad to know we fulfilled that prophecy."

"Mm-hmm, now back to what we were discussing. I wanna go out tonight and drink something and dance with you, Mr. Ross."

"Then let's do it."

***

That night, we went to a Cajun restaurant in Hot Springs that I'd heard about on the radio. There was good food, live music, and a crowd of lively people surrounding us. I dressed up in a multicolored, short sundress that clung to my hips like my body was made for it. I also wore a pair of yellow sandals, and my make-up was flawless. Thanks to my cousin, who'd re-braided my hair when I was home for my grandmother's funeral, my hair was flawless, too.

And Michael? I had never, *ever* seen anything as gorgeous as he was that night. He was a sight to see in jeans and a t-shirt, but that night—in his slacks, dress shirt, and sport coat—he was too fine for words. He captured the attention of nearly every woman in the place, and a couple of men, too. Whoever first coined the phrase "tall, dark, and handsome" must have had the foresight to know that one day Michael Ross would walk the earth, because those words most definitely described him to a tee.

I enjoyed the night out with him. My phone didn't ring once, so I was able to focus only on the present moment, on Michael Ross and how he made me feel. I even let myself wonder what a future with him would be like, what it would be like to live in a house with him and my boys, to eat dinner with him every evening, to sleep in his arms every night. He was strong, yet gentle, and I knew he'd get along well with the boys, and they really seemed to like him. Well, it was either that, or they were just amazed at him being an Indian or in awe of his stature. He was so tall and his shoulders were so wide that the average person felt small around him. He must've seemed like a giant to my sons.

As I watched him focus on the band while tapping his foot to the music, I wondered why God saw fit to send him into my life. After all I'd done, the men I'd slept with, the horrible things I'd said to and wished upon Bryan and Lamar Parker, did I even deserve a man like Michael Ross? Didn't he deserve better than me?

Michael turned and smiled at me. This time, I didn't turn away. I just smiled back at him. I wasn't ashamed of watching him or looking at him anymore. On the contrary, I felt like I needed to concentrate on him, to commit his face to my memory, so that when

I fell asleep that night, I could ensure that my dreams would be of him and only of him. But then again, he'd been the subject of my dreams since the first time I saw his beautiful body in the moonlight. No, I was staring at him because I loved him. That was it. I really and truly loved him.

When we made it back to Cook Lake, the only thought in my mind was that I didn't want to spend a single minute of the rest of my life away from him.

"Stay with me tonight," I whispered as we stood on my front porch in each other's arms.

He slid his fingertip down the bridge of my nose. "On your sofa? In your guest bed?" he asked.

I reached up and slowly kissed him. "You can sleep wherever you want to and not necessarily in those two places."

He leaned in close, letting his lips brush my ear as he spoke. "If you mean what I think you mean, then I should warn you. I'm just like a wolf. When I mate, I mate for life. So, some things will have to change before we can do that."

"Really, now? So what are you trying to say, Mr. Ross?"

"You don't know what I'm saying, Ms. Tooley?"

"Unh-uh. You're gonna have to break it down for me."

He gently rubbed his finger across my bottom lip and softly kissed my neck. "Mm… I need to go get something, and then I'll be right back so that I can, uh… break it down for you," he whispered.

I kissed him again. "Hurry."

"Don't worry, I will. I love you, Carla."

"I love you, too."

I opened the front door and nearly floated into the cabin, closing the door behind me. I leaned against it, closed my eyes, and sighed. Then I smiled as I wrapped my arms around myself. I pushed away from the door, and as I made my way to my bedroom, felt someone grab me. Before I could scream, the person covered my mouth.

"You should've locked your door," Bryan said as he dragged me back to the door and locked it himself.

25

"Turn Me Loose"

I sat on the sofa and stared at Bryan, who was sitting on the coffee table in front of me. He was leaning forward with his wild eyes fixed on me. He was so close to me that I could feel his breath on my face. I could smell his breath, too. He'd been drinking.

"Before you ask, the boys are fine. They're with my mother," he said.

"Why are you here? How did you find me?" I asked, praying that my mother or father hadn't told him where I was.

He gave me a smirk, reached into the back pocket of his jeans, and unearthed a folded envelope. "Before you so rudely hung up on me this morning, I was trying to tell you about this letter I received from my insurance company. It says here that you were treated for a spontaneous abortion." He looked up at me. "Evidently, you gave them my insurance information by mistake. This letter is a denial of payment, since you are no longer covered under my policy."

Damn, I thought. *How could I make a mistake like that?* I stared at the letter. "That doesn't explain how you got this address."

"I called the insurance company to see what this was about. The lady I spoke to gladly gave me the contact information that the hospital had on record for you—including your little temporary address."

"She had no right to do that. That's illegal."

He shrugged. "It is, but she gave it to me, anyway. Maybe it was my charm. And I *am* a doctor."

"A *dentist*."

"At any rate, why'd you lie about being in Missouri with Marli? I had a right to know where you were, Carla."

I frowned at him. "Why? So you can rape me again?"

He cocked his head to the side. "I didn't rape you. I just took what was mine in the eyes of the law and God."

"You had no right to do that to me, Bryan. I don't care what that crazy mind of yours is telling you. You had no right!"

"Let's not argue, Carla. I didn't come here to argue."

"Why *did* you come?"

"I came to find out whose baby you lost."

I sighed and wished he would turn his head. The smell of liquor on his breath was nauseating. "What difference does that make? It died. I had a miscarriage"

He slapped the envelope against the palm of his hand. "Whose baby was it?! Was it mine?!"

"Is this all you came here for? To find out whose baby I was carrying?"

"Yes!"

"It's none of your business."

He threw the envelope at me. It landed in my lap. "Tell me!"

"Why?"

"Because I have a right to know! You are my wife!"

"No, I'm not, Bryan. I'm *not* your wife! We. Are. Divorced. Get that through your head! We are over! I don't have to tell you *anything*. I don't even have to talk to you anymore!"

"I didn't want a divorce, and you know it! You're trying to throw me away, but you can't just throw me away, Carla. You can't just erase all those years of marriage."

"You're right. I can't erase something you already erased. You erased our marriage the moment you decided to cheat on me with Lamar Parker."

"I have apologized for that! I tried to make it up to you! What more can I do?"

"Move on."

"I can't. I love you."

"You didn't love me enough to stop seeing Lamar, to stop *sleeping* with him. I think you're here because of what happened between him and his wife. Did he send you here?"

"Send me here? You make it sound like I'm his woman or something."

"Oh, I'm sorry. Is he the woman or you? I get confused about these things."

His facial expression changed so quickly, I almost thought I was watching some sort of on-screen transformation—like a man morphing into a werewolf. His eyes narrowed, and his nostrils flared, and before I could even think about screaming, he pounced on me. He clutched my neck, cutting off my air supply. I reached up and dug my fingernails into the flesh of his fingers, and he quickly released me only to slap me on the cheek so hard that it felt like someone had lit a match on my skin.

I yelped as I grabbed my cheek. He stood over me, his crotch even with my face. I reached for him, squeezing his tender parts as hard as I could, and he collapsed to the floor with a wail. I jumped up from the sofa and bolted toward the door.

"You better come back here!" he screamed.

I kept running until I hit the door. I fumbled with the lock, and when I finally managed to unlock it, I heard Bryan's lumbering footsteps as he hobbled toward me. I yanked the door open, ran onto the porch and down the steps, slamming right into Michael.

Michael dropped whatever was in his hands and grabbed my arms. "What's going on?!" he shouted.

"My ex-hus-husband is in there. He-he-he hit me."

Without saying another word, Michael pulled me toward his house. He opened his door and led me inside. "Sit down," he said.

I sat down and wrapped my arms around my body and hung my head and tried not to cry. I couldn't think, didn't know what to feel. But I was glad Michael was standing in front of my cabin when I ran outside, and I was glad to be in the safety of his place.

When he returned to the living room, there was a rifle in his hand—*a big, long rifle*. I jumped to my feet. "You have a gun?! You never told me you had a gun!"

"That's another one of those rare instances when you didn't ask," he said.

"What... what are you going to do with it?!"

"Nothing as long as he leaves," he replied as he unlocked and opened his front door.

"Wait!" I yelled as I followed him out onto his porch. "Wait, please, *please* don't shoot him."

"I won't unless I have to. Go back inside. Call the police."

"What?"

"Call the police, Carla."

I froze. I knew that calling the police was the right thing to do, but I couldn't do it. I just couldn't get Bryan in trouble like that.

"Carla!" Michael shouted.

I looked up at him and slowly shook my head. "I can't. I can't do that to him."

He lowered his gun and gave me a questioning look. "You *can't*? The man broke into your home and assaulted you!"

"He didn't break in. The door was unlocked."

He released an exasperated sigh. "Did he have permission to enter your home? Did you invite him in?"

I dropped my eyes. "No."

"Then call the police! You can't let him get away with hurting you again. He won't stop unless you make him." He moved closer to me and rested his hand on my cheek. "Call the police, Carla. My phone is on the kitchen table."

I nodded. "Okay."

I hurried back inside his cabin and grabbed the phone, but before I could dial the nine, let alone the two ones, I heard Bryan shout, "You gonna shoot me, Tonto?!"

I dropped the phone and hurried back out onto the porch to find

Michael standing on the ground, a few feet away from Bryan, with his rifle pointed at him.

"M... Michael, what are you doing? What's going on?" I asked.

"You gonna stand there and let this man point a gun at me like I'm a criminal, Carla?" Bryan asked.

"You *are* a criminal," Michael said calmly.

"Go to hell! You don't know me!" Bryan yelled.

"I don't have any plans of going to hell, but I will send you there if you're not careful," Michael replied.

"Michael, put the gun down," I said.

Michael glanced at me. "Why?"

"I don't want anyone to get hurt."

"If he leaves, I won't hurt him."

I shifted my eyes to Bryan. "Please leave, Bryan. *Please*."

"Tell me if the baby was mine, and I'll go."

I sighed. "I don't know what good it's gonna do for you to know that. I don't know what difference it makes, but yes, it was your baby."

He just stood there and stared at me. I couldn't tell if he was mad or happy or upset or indifferent until he spoke again. "You did something to make yourself lose it, didn't you? You killed my baby!"

I shook my head and backed up against the outer wall of Michael's cabin. "No, Bryan. It just happened. I didn't even know I was pregnant until the doctor told me I had a miscarriage."

"You really don't owe him an explanation, Carla," Michael interjected.

"You need to stay the hell out of this! This is between me and my wife," Bryan hissed.

"*Ex*-wife," Michael countered.

"Look, I told you what you wanted to know. Now, please leave. I really don't want you to get hurt, Bryan, but I do know that Michael will hurt you before he lets you hurt me," I said.

Bryan just stood there and stared at me. Michael kept the gun trained on him.

"Please leave, Bryan. Call me later, and we'll talk," I begged, desperate to prevent a tragedy from occurring.

Even in the dimness of the night, I could see Bryan's eyes light up. "Talk about what?" he asked.

"Whatever you want to talk about. Just… please leave, okay?"

He hesitated, then nodded and began to walk away from the cabins. He stopped by my vehicle and kicked one of the tires before turning onto Cook Road, where I assumed he'd parked his car. I wondered if we'd passed right by it without noticing it.

I released a breath and closed my eyes for a second. When I opened them, Michael was walking over to my yard, picking up a bouquet of flowers I hadn't noticed lying on the ground—lavender. That must've been what I knocked out of his hands when I ran into him. He must've walked into the forest and picked them shortly after we arrived. That was probably what he was doing while Bryan was holding me hostage inside of my cabin.

I went into his cabin, to his living room, and waited for him. As soon as he walked inside, he handed me the bouquet of beautiful, dirty flowers and left the room. After several minutes of waiting for him to return to the living room, I walked through the cabin and found him sitting in the kitchen with his elbows on the table, his head in his hands.

I sat across from him and almost immediately noticed a ring box sitting in the middle of the table. I eyed it as I said, "Thank you for the flowers."

He nodded without lifting his head to look at me.

"Are you okay?" I asked.

He looked up at me. His eyes followed mine to the ring box. "The police been here yet?" he asked, ignoring my question.

I tore my eyes away from the ring box and focused all of my attention on Michael. "No... I, uh... I never called them."

He sighed loudly and sat up straight in his chair. "That's what I thought."

"I was going to, but then I heard Bryan say something about you shooting him, and I just wanted to make sure nothing tragic happened."

"You think I would shoot him in cold blood?"

"No."

"Then what were you so afraid of?"

I shrugged. "I don't know. I guess I was afraid Bryan would do something to provoke you into shooting him. I can't stand him, but—"

"But he's the father of your sons. I know. You've made that *unforgettably* clear."

"Michael—"

"Look, I'm tired, and I need to check my blood sugar. Stress always makes it go haywire. You're welcome to stay here tonight if you're too afraid to go back to your place. You can have the guest bed."

"The guest bed?" As he stood to leave, I grabbed his arm. "Wait, is… is that a ring? Is that what you meant by things changing?" I asked, pointing to the box.

He stared down at me with uncharacteristically emotionless eyes as he picked up the box and shoved it into his pants pocket. "It's nothing."

"Michael—"

"Goodnight, Carla."

That was it. No kiss, no hug, not even a glance in my direction. I had really messed up.

26

"Late Nights & Early Mornings"

I took Michael up on his offer and spent the night in his guest bedroom. The next morning, I fixed breakfast, and we ate together in complete silence. He didn't as much as glance in my direction throughout the entire meal. When he left for his run, I headed back over to my cabin to find all four of the tires on my vehicle flat, the handiwork of Bryan, no doubt. I didn't have the mental capacity to deal with that. My head was in a fog from Bryan waiting for me the night before. I was half-afraid he'd be there that morning, but thank God, he wasn't. Then there was Michael—sweet, caring, noble Michael. He was running low on patience with me. That, I could clearly tell. I was running out of patience with myself, too. Why was I still trying to protect Bryan? Did I still love him? No, that couldn't be it. There was no way I could love someone who hurt me the way he did, someone intent on hurting me again.

Then, what was it? Why was I protecting him, almost against my own will?

I sat on the side of my bed and eyed the journal and rape information Marli had sent me. Maybe it was time to read that stuff and get a better handle on my situation. Maybe something in that literature could offer me an explanation as to why I was so bent on protecting Bryan, of all people. I sat there for the better part of that morning, reading pamphlet after pamphlet, learning about the different types of sexual assault and the effects of them all. Partner Rape—that's what had happened to me. And among the effects, I found two that fit me to a tee: post-traumatic stress disorder and Stockholm syndrome. The post-traumatic stress disorder would explain my fear and anxiety when it came to Bryan. Stockholm syndrome explained why I kept protecting him. I read on, devouring the information and taking notes in my journal.

I even made a list of the steps I could take to recover. First on my list was to call Marli and thank her for sending me the information. Second on my list was to share the information with Michael. Third, I would search for a counselor; fourth, I'd make an appointment to be tested for STDs. And last, I promised myself that if Bryan even walked toward me again, I was calling the police. By the time I finished studying the information and mapping out a strategy to put my life back together, I noticed that Michael's truck was gone.

It was later that afternoon when I finally heard him pull into his driveway. I was so excited about my little breakthrough that I ran from my house to catch him as he climbed out of his truck. I hugged him around the neck and kissed his cheek. He gave me an odd look, but I wasn't going to let that stop me from sharing my good news with him.

"I'm so glad you're back!" I began.

He frowned slightly. "Your tires are flat—all of them. Did you notice that?"

"Yeah, I called a little while ago, and someone is on their way to put some new ones on. Um, how's your blood sugar been?"

"It was fine this morning. I need to check it again." He turned toward his cabin.

"Wait! I need to tell you something. I have some good news. I've been reading through the information that my friend, Marli, sent me, and I know why I acted so stupid about calling the police on Bryan. I have this condition that rape victims get sometimes, but I can get help for it and—"

"Carla—"

"No, let me finish. I owe you an apology. I know I've tried your patience, and I am so sorry. I was acting stupid, trying to protect Bryan. I'm sorry, Michael. I don't want to lose you."

"Carla—"

I squeezed my eyes shut. "Please don't say it. Don't tell me that you're done with me, because I really don't think I could take that right now."

"Carla… you keep letting him hurt you over and over again. I want to be there for you, to protect you, but I don't know how to do that when you keep fighting me on it. I don't know what to think except that you don't feel the same about me as I feel about you."

"But I do. I love you, Michael."

"But I think you love *him*."

I shook my head. "No… no, I don't. I promise you I don't. I… I love *you*."

He sighed and turned his back to me. Then he turned around to face me and placed his hand gently on my cheek. "I wish I could believe you."

I placed my hand over his. "You *can*. You can believe me. I'm telling you, if Bryan even breathes toward me again, I'm calling the police on him. I promise I am."

He stared down at me for a moment, leaned in closer, and softly kissed me. "Okay, but you also have to call and report the rape."

I dropped my head. "But it's too late. There's no evidence, no pictures or anything. It'd just be my word against his."

"I know, but you still need to do it, to show him that you're not going to let him get away with what he did to you."

"O… okay. But not today. I'll do it tomorrow. I'll call the police tomorrow. I promise."

He kissed me again, took my hand, and led me into his cabin, where we spent the remainder of the day together in each other's arms.

***

I was asleep on the floor next to Michael when my cell phone woke me up. My eyes were so blurry that I couldn't see the screen well, so I decided to answer it blindly, hoping that it wasn't Bryan calling to start some more mess.

"Hello?" I said groggily as I moved Michael's arm from my waist and sat up on the floor. Almost instantly, he sat up beside me and placed his hand on my back.

"Mama, it's Derek," my son whispered.

I took the phone from my face and checked the time on the screen—3:00 A.M. Panic raced through my veins. My heart rate doubled. "Derek, what is it? What's going on?"

"I don't know. We've been here at Grandma Tina's house for like three days, and Daddy ain't even called us."

I rubbed my eyes and yawned. "Well, I'm sure he'll be back tomorrow. Did you call him?"

"Yeah. He won't answer."

"Don't worry, Derek. He'll come get you. What are you doing up so early?"

"Something is going on. Somebody came knocking at the front door a few minutes ago, and then Grandma Tina started screaming and stuff. When I went to see what was going on, she sent me back to bed. Now there's a bunch of folks here. I can hear them talking and stuff."

I frowned. "Okay, let me see what I can find out. You go back to bed. I'll talk to you later. Hey, how's Patrick?"

"He's good. Asleep."

"Good. I'll call you a little later, okay?"

"Yes, ma'am."

I hung up and tried Bryan's cell which rang straight to voicemail. I held the phone in my hand and wondered if I should call Bryan's mother since it was so early in the morning. But then again, Derek said she was already awake.

"What's going on?" Michael asked.

I shrugged. "I'm not sure. My son called and said something's going on at his grandmother's house and that he can't get in touch with my ex. I just tried to call him, and it went straight to voicemail. I have a feeling something might have happened to him. I'm… I'm gonna call his mother."

Michael nodded and watched as I dialed the number.

After several rings, a man answered the phone by shouting, "Hello!" There were several voices in the background.

"Hello? Um, may I speak with Ms. Tina Foster?" I replied.

"She can't come to the phone right now. Can I take a message?"

"Um, this is Carla, her son's ex-wife. Can I ask who I'm speaking to?"

"Carla? This is A.B. Look, are you in town? Can you come over here? You really need to come over here," said A.B., Bryan's youngest brother

I felt my chest tighten. "Why… what's going on, A.B.?"

"It's Bryan. He's been in an accident—a car accident."

I held the phone and stared straight ahead. I couldn't think for a moment. As much as he had hurt me, as much as I sometimes despised him, as angry as I was at him, I never really wanted anything bad to happen to him. Not really.

"Carla? You still there?"

"Is he… is he dead?"

"No, but it don't look good. Look, he had the accident between here and Malvern sometime last night. They're gonna airlift him to Little Rock. We need to head on up there. You coming here or you wanna meet us there? We'll bring the boys with us."

I snapped out of my trance for a second and said, "I'll meet you there. Which hospital?"

I really don't remember much of what happened after A.B. gave me the information about the hospital. I think I tried to drive myself, but Michael wouldn't let me. He drove me to Little Rock to check on my ex-husband, and the whole ride there, I felt like I was in the middle of a dream—no, a nightmare.

***

Things at the hospital were tense. I was glad to see my boys, but the staring, accusing eyes of my former in-laws, which were glued to me and Michael, were unnerving. Maybe it was wrong for him to be there, but I definitely couldn't have safely made the drive on my own, regardless of the new tires on my vehicle—that was for sure. I was just too on edge. Besides, Bryan and I were divorced. It really wasn't any of their business who I was with. But I have to admit that it was strange sitting there holding Michael's hand while waiting for word on Bryan.

Bryan's mother, who was distraught to say the least, sobbed nonstop. Her children and other relatives surrounded her, offering comfort that just didn't seem to penetrate her despair. I felt bad for her. Of all of her four children, Bryan was the most successful and definitely her favorite. Anyone could see that. I silently prayed that he would be okay for her sake as well as my boys', who both wore worried expressions on their young faces.

I tried to comfort them, but the truth was that I was worried, myself. Although we were no longer husband and wife, there was a bond between me and Bryan that still existed. I'd spent the better part of my life as either his girlfriend or his wife. I had loved him for years. In some ways, I still did, though I knew we could never be together again.

A.B. had explained that Bryan, who was drunk when he broke into my house and was still drunk when he left, had fallen asleep at the wheel and run off of the road. There were no other cars involved in the accident, but Bryan's vehicle was totaled and he had suffered great injuries, including brain damage. He was not expected to make it.

I tried to let that soak in without feeling guilty. I knew he was drunk. I shouldn't have let him drive like that, but I was afraid for him to stay—afraid of what he'd do to me and afraid of what Michael would do to him. But still, I should've stopped him. I knew I should've. And because I didn't stop him, I felt partially responsible for his accident.

"What was he doing on the highway drunk anyway?" Bryan's older sister, Pam, asked. "Who does he know up that way?"

"I don't know," Bryan's mother said. "He ain't been right since the divorce. Been doing all kinds of crazy stuff."

I dropped my eyes and squeezed Michael's hand.

"Don't you look away *now*, you heifer! You ruined my son's life, leaving him like that! You broke his heart!" his mother screamed at me.

Michael squeezed my hand and looked at me. I shook my head, knowing that he wanted to defend me. "Now is not the time to do this, Ms. Tina," I said softly. The last thing I wanted to do was to reveal the truth at that moment. I couldn't do it under those circumstances or with my sons present. And I wasn't going to let her goad me into it.

"It's time when I *say* it's time! My son is in there fighting for his life, and I know you had something to do with it. He was probably running in behind you. And you have the nerve to come here with another man. You ain't never been good enough for my boy! I just tolerated you because he loved you. Then you up and left him. You are a sorry, *sorry* woman!" she ranted.

I raised my eyes to meet hers. "Ms. Tina, you have no idea what has happened between us, but let me just say that Bryan is no saint and leave it at that."

"You talking about him when he is back there hurt and can't defend himself?!" she shrieked.

"No, ma'am. That's not what I'm doing at all." I sighed. "Look, I don't want to argue with anyone. I'm here for my boys, but I can leave. We can all leave."

Before she could reply, a doctor walked into the waiting area with an oddly blank look on his face, and before he said the words aloud, I heard them in my spirit.

Bryan was dead.

27

"I Don't Know Why, But I Do"

The sound of Ms. Tina's shrill cries followed me as Michael led me and my distraught sons from the hospital to my SUV. That sound rang in my ears as I lay in my bed between my sons, who'd cried themselves to sleep though it was only mid-morning. They were too upset to even ask about the cabin or why I wasn't in St. Louis.

As I lay there staring at the ceiling, my thoughts were of Ms. Tina and her grief as I tried to wrap my mind around what it would feel like to lose one of my boys. No matter their ages, I knew it would be a devastatingly painful thing to endure. I honestly couldn't wrap my mind around it any more than I could wrap my mind around losing my father as my sons had just lost theirs. It was all just too much to fathom.

But it was easier to ponder those things than to let the guilt I felt eat at me any more than it already was. I couldn't stop thinking about him, drunk and distraught as he left Cook Lake on foot. I couldn't get the image of him swerving along the highway and running off of the road out of my head. And I couldn't help but think that I should've stopped him. Somehow, I should've kept him from leaving. I knew he couldn't hold his liquor. He never could. I should've offered to let him sleep the booze off in my cabin, and I could've stayed with Michael. Maybe I should've just called the police and let them arrest him. I should've done something, *anything*, to stop him.

That afternoon, I eased out of bed, leaving my boys behind, and slipped past a sleeping Michael, who'd been keeping vigil on my couch. I walked into the kitchen with the idea to cook some dinner, but for the life of me, I couldn't think of anything I wanted to cook or eat. So I started the coffeemaker and took a seat at the table. I buried my face in my hands and tried to clear my mind. I was startled when I heard one of the kitchen chairs slide across the hardwood floor.

My head snapped up, and I watched as Michael took a seat across from me. "Hey. You okay?" he asked in his usual calm, even voice.

I shook my head. "I shouldn't have let him drive like that. I smelled the liquor on his breath when he was in here. I knew he was drunk. I should've stopped him."

Michael reached across the table and took my hand. "This is not your fault, Carla."

I glued my eyes to the table. "I think it is. I could've stopped him."

"Could you have stopped him from driving here drunk in the first place? He could've just as easily had a wreck on the way here."

I just shook my head. He was making sense, but in my grief, I didn't want to hear it.

"Carla, he was a grown man, an adult who made a lot of bad decisions, not the least of which was assaulting and terrorizing you. You can't let his death diminish what he did to you. You can't shoulder the blame for his actions."

"I should've listened to you, though. I should've called the police. At least then maybe he'd be in jail instead of dead."

"Don't do this to yourself. It's not going to change anything. It's just going to make things more difficult for you."

I nodded, slipped my hand out of his, and stood from the table. I walked over to the counter to pour my cup of coffee. "You probably should leave and go back to your cabin. I think I need to spend some time alone with my boys," I said with my back to him.

There was silence, and then Michael said, "Yeah… um, okay." I heard the chair slide across the floor again. "I'll be back to check on you later."

I turned to face him. "Okay."

He walked over to me and planted a kiss on my cheek. "I love you," he said softly.

I gave him a small smile. "I love you, too."

I sighed as I watched him walk out of my back door.

The balance of the day was spent cooking random stuff from my kitchen. I basically just cooked up everything I had—chicken, steak, potatoes, beans, macaroni and cheese. The boys were appreciative and seemed to enjoy the variety. I still had no appetite, so I just watched them eat. They were obviously still sad, and I knew it would take a while for them to get better, but I also knew that one day they *would* get better. There wasn't a doubt in my mind about that. Resilience is one of the good things about children. Since time heals wounds, and they were only beginning their lives, I knew their wounds would eventually heal, and they would move on. I wasn't so sure if things would be that easy for me.

"I miss Daddy," Patrick said as he took a bite of macaroni and cheese.

"I know you do, baby. I know you do. I wish there was something I could do to make things better. I wish I could bring him back for you." I shifted my eyes to Derek. "For both of you."

Derek didn't look up from his plate as he said, "I wonder where he was going? Why'd he leave us with Grandma Tina for so long?"

I froze. I wasn't sure what I should tell them, if anything. Would it make a difference for them to know he'd been on his way home from seeing me? Would it ease their pain? As I weighed my options, I realized I'd have to tell them why he came, that he'd entered my cabin illegally. I'd have to tell them about the miscarriage. I'd have to tell them everything, the whole truth. I just couldn't see how that would help them heal. I couldn't tell them the truth. Not then. Not so soon after Bryan's death.

"None of that matters, baby. What matters is that your daddy loved you and Patrick. I don't want you two to ever forget that. I want you to remember how he lived, not how he died. I want you to remember the times you had together, okay?"

"Yes, ma'am," they said in unison.

A couple of minutes later, there was a knock at the back door. I knew it was Michael, and when I opened the door, I gave him the best smile I could as I eased outside. I shut the door behind me and said, "Hey."

"Hey," he said as he pulled me into a hug. "Everything okay?"

I nodded as I slowly backed out of his arms. "Yeah, they're eating right now."

"How about you?"

I shrugged. "I guess I'm all right. How are you? Get any rest?"

"I'm fine. I was thinking about taking a swim this evening. Your boys know how to swim? Think they'll want to join me?"

"Um, not tonight. I think they're still tired from everything that's happened."

"Oh, okay."

We stood there in awkward silence for a moment. Then I said, "Well, I guess I better get back to them. You want me to fix you a plate to take with you?"

He looked a little disappointed as he said, "Uh, no, thank you. I'll just check on you in the morning."

I reached up and kissed his cheek. "Thank you. See you later."

He looked at me for a moment. "Yeah. See you later."

I spent the next couple of days basically dodging Michael, meeting him at the door with lame excuses, or just plain ignoring him. I felt kind of bad about it, but if I was really truthful with myself, I'd have to admit that things between us had been moving too fast anyway. All of those declarations of love were not even real, were they? How could they be? We barely knew each other. Besides, I needed to focus all of my attention on my boys. Bryan's funeral was that next weekend, and we'd have to go back home. I had almost decided to pack everything up and leave Cook Lake for good when I went back for Bryan's funeral. Cook Lake was a fairy tale world that was now ruined. It was time for me to step back into reality.

So, the night before the funeral, I packed up my clothes, threw away the leftover food, and tried to tidy up the place and put it back the way it was when I arrived. Before dawn the next morning, I loaded everything into my truck and dropped the key in Mrs. Cook's mailbox with a note thanking her. Then I drove back to Pine Bluff, leaving the serenity of Cook Lake and Michael Ross behind.

***

It was a sad funeral, just like most funerals of loved ones who were snatched away in their prime. Bryan's family was in shambles. My boys cried throughout the entire service. I even shed some tears. The Parkers where there, evidently reunited now. Deacon Parker looked stricken, his wife looked exhausted. As I sat in the packed church and listened to person after person speak kind, exalting words about Bryan, I felt a sorrow creep deep inside of me. It wasn't necessarily a sorrow borne out of his death. It was more of a sorrow borne out of the fact that I felt a little relief along with the guilt that seemed to constantly seize me. At least now I didn't have to worry about him hurting me again. He couldn't rape me from the grave.

I looked around at the people crowding the sanctuary and realized that the only people in that place who truly knew who and what Bryan really was were me and the Parkers. We, alone, knew his secrets. And I, alone, knew what he was truly capable of. I was the only person who'd met the monster that lived inside of his troubled soul. I believed I was the one person he ever truly loved besides our sons, but the amount of love he'd given me was directly equivalent to the amount of pain he'd inflicted upon me.

As soon as the word "love" entered my brain, Michael's face appeared before me, his chocolate eyes boring into mine, his slight smile warming my soul. I missed him, and I missed Cook Lake, although I'd only been away from there for a few hours. I shook myself a little and told myself to focus on the service. There was no need in me longing for Michael Ross. We'd never be together again. I'd made sure of that when I left him behind without even saying goodbye.

28

"My Heart"

Two weeks after Bryan's funeral, I sat in my old bedroom at my parents' house and prepared to go to Bryan's lawyer's office for the reading of his will. As it turned out, I still couldn't stand to be in my apartment, despite the fact that Bryan was gone. Every time I walked into my bedroom, I thought about the rape and the baby I carried as a result—then lost. And those memories were just too much for me. It was just easier for me to be at my parents' house, and the boys didn't seem to mind being there at all.

I hadn't spoken with Michael since I left Cook Lake, but not from a lack of trying on his part. He'd called every single day since the day I left. I just hadn't answered the phone. I couldn't. I couldn't hear his voice. I couldn't think about loving him. I needed to clear my mind of all of that and move on with my life.

As I reached down to buckle the strap on my sandal, my cell phone rang. I smiled as Marli's name appeared on the screen.

"Hello?" I answered.

"Hey! What's going on?"

"Nothing. Getting ready to go hear Bryan's will be read."

"Oh, yeah. You told me about that. Hey, I was wondering, who paid for his funeral? I mean, no one's been awarded any life insurance or anything, right?"

"Right. Well, Bryan's funeral was prepaid. We both prepaid for our funerals years ago to spare either of us from having to make the arrangements in the event that one of us died."

"Oh, I see. Well, I still wish you'd told me about the funeral beforehand. I would've come, you know? I knew Bryan for years. No matter what happened recently, I would've liked to have paid my respects."

I sighed softly. "I know, and I'm so sorry. Things were just so messed up, I couldn't think straight. My only thoughts were of my boys, you know?"

"I understand. I guess that's how other things got messed up, too, huh?"

This time I sighed heavily into the phone. "What are you throwing out hints about now?"

"You know what I'm hinting about. What's going on with Michael?"

"What do you mean?"

"Really? You wanna play dumb now?"

"I'm not playing dumb. There's nothing going on with Michael."

"That's what I'm talking about. There really is nothing going on. *Nothing at all.* You just left the poor man without even a goodbye."

I frowned. "How would you know that?" I hadn't shared that bit of information with her.

"Because he called me sounding all confused."

"Called you?! How'd he get your number?"

"He got it when y'all were here for your grandmother's funeral. I gave it to him in case something like this happened."

"Something like what?" I asked as I dug in my purse for my lip gloss.

"Something like you losing your doggone mind."

I rolled my eyes. "Whatever. I haven't lost my mind. Losing my mind was thinking I'd fallen in love with a man I'd known for less than a month."

It was Marli's turn to sigh.

"What're you sighing for?"

"You sound like me."

"No, I don't."

"Yeah, you do. Do you remember when you blessed me out about the way I was acting with Chris?"

"This is different."

"No, it's not! What's different about a good man wanting you and you pushing him away? Sounds like me and Chris in the past to me."

"Look, I've got to concentrate on my sons, Marli. You can't fault me for that. Neither can Michael."

"You're punishing yourself."

I shook my head. "You have definitely been talking to Michael. He said something similar."

"He said you feel guilty about letting Bryan leave, because you knew he was drunk."

"Well, I *do* feel bad about that, but that's not why I can't be with Michael."

"Then, what is it?"

I hesitated then walked over to my bedroom door and shut it. "For one, I've never been tested for AIDS or any other STDs. Bryan got me pregnant. He could've given me something else, too," I whispered, finally getting something off of my chest that had been bothering me for weeks.

"Well, first of all, go get tested. Second, didn't you tell me that he married his late wife knowing she was HIV positive? No matter your status, you know it won't change how he feels about you."

"I know that he'll still want me, but I'm still afraid."

"Afraid to get tested?"

"Yes."

"You've got to do it, Carla. You've *got* to get tested."

I took a deep breath and blinked back tears. "I know. Just… just pray that I'll find the strength to do it and to face the results."

"I will. I will definitely pray. But you've got to stop shutting Michael out. He really cares about you," she said softly.

A knock at my door startled me. "Carla, someone's at the front door for you!" my mother said.

"Um, I gotta go, Marli. Talk to you later?"

"Yeah, I'll call you tonight."

I ended the call and opened the door. "Someone?" I said as I squeezed past my mother.

"Mm-hmm, someone named Michael," she replied.

I stopped mid-stride and turned to look at her. She was wearing this strange smirk on her face. I frowned slightly as I continued walking to the front door. Sure enough, standing there on the other side was Michael, *my Michael*. I walked out onto the porch and softly shut the door behind me.

"Michael... what are you doing here? How'd you know I'd be here?" Almost as soon as the words left my mouth, I knew the answer, and he quickly confirmed my suspicions.

He stared down at me, nearly piercing my soul with his eyes. "You didn't give me any choice. You won't answer or return any of my calls, so I called your friend, Marli, and she told me where you were staying."

"Why? Why are you here?"

His eyes stretched wide. "I'm here because I love you, and I was worried about you. You're shutting me out of your life, and I want to know why."

I shook my head. "I'm not shutting you out. I just... the time is not right for us, Michael. I need to be here for my boys. I need to concentrate on them, and there are other things I need to take care of. I never should've started up with you in the first place."

His brow furrowed. "Started up with me? You don't love me?" He placed his hand on his chest.

I began to wring my hands. "I do. I do love you, but that doesn't matter right now."

He backed away from me a bit. "That doesn't matter?" He slowly lifted his eyebrows. "You're scared. That's it. You're scared of being hurt, aren't you?"

I dropped my eyes. "No, I'm not. I just told you, I need to devote all of my attention to my boys, and I need to get myself together."

"Carla, look at me."

I fixed my gaze on his beautiful face.

"You're just afraid. Why are you so afraid to love me? Don't you know there's no fear in love?"

"Yes, there is," I whispered.

"Not when the love is real." He raised his hand and gently placed it on my cheek. Then he leaned in and kissed me so deeply that I almost lost my footing for a moment. "I love you, Carla. With everything that I am, *I love you.* I was made to love you, and you were made to love me. Let me back in. Let me back into your heart. *Please.*"

I wanted to love him. I wanted to grab him and never let him go, but instead, I shook my head as a single tear rolled down my cheek. "I can't."

He stared down at me with a sadness that clouded his eyes, then he pressed a feather-light kiss onto my forehead. He closed his eyes, took a deep breath, and walked away.

I stood there and watched as he backed his truck out of my parents' driveway. Tears raced down my cheeks as I whispered, "I love you so much. I'm so sorry."

"He'll wait, but he won't wait forever," a voice said. I wiped my face and turned to see my mother standing in the doorway.

"How would you know that? Did it come to you in a dream or something? You're overdue to give me some supernatural advice," I said sarcastically.

Mama stepped out onto the porch and rested her hand on my shoulder. "Baby, not everything has to be supernatural. Some things come from good old common sense. That's a good man, but even a good man has his limits. You can make him wait if you want to, but you better hope you don't make him wait too long and end up losing him."

As I watched her walk back into the house, I knew she was right. But Michael was right, too. I was scared.

29

"Upside Down"

If I wasn't already confused enough, my visit to Bryan's lawyer really left my mind in a tangle. With the exception of one life insurance policy, of which his mother was beneficiary, Bryan left everything to me—the house we'd once shared, his car, his share of the dental practice, his bank accounts, and two life insurance policies. After the will was read, I just sat there for several minutes, trying to understand. Bryan's mother and other relatives had long left before I finally stood from my seat and stumbled toward the door.

"Are you okay?" the lawyer, Mr. Ramble, asked.

I glanced around the room, and once I realized I was the only person in the office besides him, I said, "I don't understand."

He frowned slightly. "What don't you understand? Do you need me to go over the will with you again?"

I slowly shook my head. "No, I mean, I understand what the will says, I just don't understand *why*."

His expression softened. "Have a seat," he offered.

I moved backward a little and slid into one of the empty chairs that faced his desk.

"The 'why' of all of this is that Dr. Foster loved you. When he came in to draw up this will shortly after your divorce was final, I thought he was going to remove you. Instead, he told me he wanted to be sure that you would always be provided for. He felt responsible for the dissolution of your marriage, and you know what he told me?"

I shook my head.

"He told me that it was his job to make sure you and the boys were taken care of—in life and in the event of his death. He felt that you would always be his wife and he your husband, despite the divorce."

I sat there and stared at my late ex-husband's lawyer and fought the desire to burst into tears. Bryan had loved me, and despite his love, he'd hurt me. I wasn't sure which reality injured me the most, and the confusion made my brain feel like it was floating in boiling water. "Um… thank you for sharing that with me," I finally said.

"You're welcome," he replied with a warm smile.

Instead of heading straight back to my parents' house, I found myself merging onto the highway that led to Garland County. I had no idea why. Maybe I just needed to revisit the serenity of Cook Lake in the wake of this newest revelation about Bryan. Or maybe, just maybe, I needed to see Michael. I drove with tears in my eyes and turmoil in my heart. Bryan had loved me. Michael *still* loved me. And in a way, I loved them both. But Bryan was gone, and even if he had lived, there was no way we could've reconciled, because he'd raped me. As that thought hit my mind, my foot hit the brake, jerking my car to a halt in the middle of an empty stretch of highway.

That thought and the realization of what it meant raced back and forth in my mind. *He raped me. He pinned me down and forced my legs open. I said no. I begged him to stop. He raped me. And now, I'll never understand why…*

I hadn't faced it before. Not really. It had merely been a known fact tucked somewhere in the back of my head, where I'd pushed it. I was aware of it—lived in fear of it happening again despite the fact that he was gone, but I had never really faced it head-on until that moment in my vehicle on my way to my serenity.

I flung the door open and stepped out onto the steamy highway pavement, heat slapping me in the face almost instantly. I covered my ears and screamed as horrible thoughts repeated over and over again in my mind like the chorus of an annoying song—*he raped me. Bryan raped me. He raped me. And now he's dead. He's dead. He's dead. He's dead because I wanted him dead. I wished him dead. I didn't stop him from dying.*

"No!" I screamed.

A car whizzed by on the opposite side, the driver blaring his horn as he passed me. I stared after the car, glad that the voices in my head had stopped. Then, as soon as the silence of the lonely highway returned, so did the voices. *He raped you. You killed him. He raped you.*

I covered my ears again, and I screamed and yelled myself hoarse. Cars passed by me on both sides. People craned their necks and blew their horns. And I just stood there with covered ears, and screamed. I didn't stop when the state trooper's car pulled up behind mine. I didn't move a muscle when he approached me. And when he escorted me to the back of his cruiser, I didn't shed a tear.

***

Just a few months earlier, no one could've told me I'd end up where I was at that moment. Who would've guessed that I'd be locked up in a psychiatric hospital, writing in my journal while sitting on the side of a bed in a sterile, white room? Well, at least I didn't have a roommate. Lucky for me, I had a private room, but having a private room didn't take away the sting of having to be away from my sons. Having a private room didn't fill the empty spaces in my heart. Having a private room couldn't help me regain my sanity.

Then again, I definitely wasn't the craziest person residing at the Ida M. Forks Psychiatric Center. No, not by a country mile. But I had my issues; that was for sure. My little mental breakdown in the middle of Highway 270 had bought me a ticket directly into that place, and even *I* had to admit that I needed to be there. Too much had happened to me. As tough as I thought myself to be, being raped by someone you loved and once trusted was a lot to try to deal with on your own. Losing an unexpected baby didn't help matters. And bearing the guilt of someone's death was enough to make an Ironman World Champion break.

I took my treatment seriously, listened to the counselors, and downed the pills they gave me without any argument. I wanted to leave that place the first chance I got. But more than that, I wanted to leave a changed woman. Yet, I knew it would take more than what the people in that facility could do for me to bring that about. It would take God. It would take me finding my way back to Him. I'd been lost for so long, had been wandering around in the wilderness since the day I caught Bryan with Lamar Parker. As Michael had once described himself, I'd been homeless since my marriage exploded before my eyes. It was time for me to go home. It was time for the prodigal daughter to return and stop wallowing in a self-constructed mud hole. If I didn't know anything else, I knew that.

So, in between individual counseling sessions, family counseling sessions with my sons, group counseling sessions with other patients, pill calls, and recreation time, I opened my Bible, and I read the Word with open eyes and an open heart. I fell on my knees, and I prayed. Marli would call every other day and pray with and for me. I confided in my mother—gave her full disclosure of what had happened between me and Bryan, and she prayed a prayer over the phone that surely knocked the breath out of Ol' Slewfoot.

    I forgave Bryan, and I forgave myself. The holes in my heart began to close, leaving scars that were thick but painless. I began to heal. I confronted all of the pain that I had kept bottled up inside of me. I lifted my hands and gave that pain to Jesus. Yes, I began to heal.

30
"All I Ever Think About"

After three weeks in the psychiatric facility, I was released to once again face the world. The first thing I did was quit my job. There was no sense in pretending I was going to be able to go back any time soon, so I went to the hospital and turned in my resignation, making my leave of absence a permanent one. I knew I'd be fine financially. I still had a pretty nice amount of money in my savings account, and that, plus the insurance money Bryan had left me, would keep me afloat for a while.

The second thing I did was hire a couple of my cousins to pack up me and Bryan's old house. I'd told Bryan's family that they could have Bryan's stuff, and they had already removed the possessions they wanted. So my cousins packed up what was left and put it in storage for me until I had the strength to sift through it myself. I was better, but I wasn't quite ready to dig through the remnants of Bryan's life. Not yet.

The next thing I did was put our house on the market and pray that it would sell. I planned to add the money from the sale of the house to the boys' college fund. After taking care of the business end of things, I started to work on my personal life. I spent as much time as I could with the boys before the school year began, and I made sure we never missed a Sunday at our new church. I couldn't go back to the old one. Though I felt better, I knew I wasn't going to be able to stomach seeing Lamar Parker sitting on the deacon's bench every Sunday. And I wasn't going to be able to look into his lovely wife's eyes and see a reflection of myself.

I even found us a new house. Well, it wasn't exactly a new house. It was actually Grandma Tooley's house that she'd had to abandon when it became dangerous for her to live alone. It sat outside of town on the bank of the Arkansas River. It was small and plain—not luxurious or fancy at all—but it was so peaceful. When Daddy took me to check it out, I knew it was just what the boys and I needed.

So I settled into my riverside home—me and my growing sons—and I wrote in my journal about my feelings, just as I had been taught to by my counselors. I read some of the self-help books Marli had sent me while I was in the psychiatric center. I sat on my little porch and prayed to God every morning as the river crept by. I cooked meals and taught my sons how to fish. I slept well at night, and I smiled as the sun shone on my face in the day time. Things were good, but even in the peace and calm that enveloped me, I knew something… *someone* was missing. That someone stayed on my mind almost constantly. I just didn't know what to do to fix things.

***

"You're a hard woman to catch up with," Marli said after I answered the phone.

"What do you mean? Did I miss a call from you or something?"

"Carla, I have been calling you every day for a week! I even left some messages. What's going on? Are you okay?"

"I'm fine. I guess it's the cell reception out here on the river. I'm surprised this call came through."

"The river, huh? You still liking it out there?"

"Yeah, I love it here. It's so peaceful. I go for walks every day. And did I tell you I got a boat? Sometimes I get in that boat and just sit on the water."

"That's nice, Carla. I'm glad you're doing good. You really had me worried for a minute there."

"Yeah, I had myself worried."

"Yeah. Well, Christmas is right around the corner. You got any plans? If not, you and the boys are welcome to come and celebrate with us."

"No, I think we'll stay here and celebrate in our new home."

"Oh, okay. Um, Carla... can I talk to you about something?" she asked gently, like she was afraid I'd shatter if she spoke too strongly.

"Marli, I'm not insane anymore, so you can change your tone of voice. What's on your mind?"

"Um... well, I know you have worked hard to get to where you are, and I am so proud of you. But I've noticed something, and I just feel like it's my duty to share this with you... as your friend."

I leaned forward on my sofa. It was almost time to drive into town and pick the boys up from school. "What is it?"

"Do you realize what you've done, what you're *doing*?"

I frowned. "What are you talking about, Marli?"

"I'm talking about the house on the water, the boat, the walks. Carla, you have never been one who was so in tune with nature."

"Well, damn! I've changed. Is that a crime?" I said, feeling more than a little irritated.

"I think you're trying to relive your time on the lake, and I can understand why. But there's one problem."

I sighed. "And what would that be, Dr. King?"

"Carla, don't be like that."

"Look, Marli, I've got to leave in a second to go pick up the boys. I'm sure I'm gonna drop this call the moment I climb into my truck, so say what you need to say."

"Okay... um, Carla, you can't relive that time on the lake without Michael. It's been months. You've punished yourself enough. He loves you, and you love him. You need to call him."

I held the phone and shut my eyes, but I didn't say a word.

"Carla, did I ever thank you?" Marli asked.

I frowned, wondering what in the world she was talking about now. "For what?"

"For convincing me to call Chris and come clean about my pregnancy."

"Well... you're welcome."

"But more than that, I need to thank you for letting God use you to take me to St. Louis. If God hadn't planted that travel job idea in your head, and you hadn't planted it in mine, I might never have met the love of my life. God sent me to St. Louis so that Chris could find me. He sent you to Cook Lake so that Michael could find you. It was divine intervention, Carla."

"Marli—"

"You've been tested *several* times in the last few months. You are disease free. You have no more excuses. Don't waste this blessing that God has given you, and stop wasting time. *Call him.*"

I drew in a deep breath and released it. "I need to go now, Marli," I said.

"I know you don't want to hear this, but you *need* to hear it. *Call him.*"

A single tear escaped my eye. "I've gotta go."

"Okay, I love you, Carla. Please think about what I said."

"I will. I really will."

After we hung up, I sat there for a moment and reflected on what she'd said to me as Monsieur Nov softly serenaded me on my stereo. She was right, of course. I had spent all of my time trying to relive my experience at the lake, trying to replicate what it felt like to be with Michael. His face occupied my dreams. His touch felt as if it was tattooed on my skin. Every word he'd ever said to me nearly constantly echoed in my mind. I even had ancestral DNA testing done so that I could learn of my past like he'd suggested. The results had shocked and delighted me. I was of a majority African descent, of course, with a smidgen of European heritage and five percent Native American. Imagine that.

A short while later, I left to pick up my sons. On the bridge that straddled the Arkansas River, I pulled out my phone and dialed Michael's number. When the tones blared in my ear and the computerized voice announced that the number had been disconnected and was no longer in service, my heart fell.

31

"A Couple Of Forevers"

It took me a little over a week to recover from learning that Michael's phone number was no longer valid. Up until that point, I had placed Michael in a pocket inside of my heart and left him there with the belief that I could reach in and pull him out anytime I was ready. The thought never occurred to me that his number would change, that he wouldn't be somewhere waiting by his phone for my call. The reality of the situation was like a bomb exploding in my brain. It was at that moment, the moment I heard the three tones blaring from my phone into my ear, followed by, "We're sorry, the number you are trying to reach has been disconnected and is no longer in service," that I realized how big a mistake I had made in pushing Michael away.

The only thought in my mind was that he was gone for good. He was gone, he was done with me, and I would never see him or touch him again. I ruined things between us. I destroyed things before they really had a chance to start. I was at fault, and to be honest, I couldn't blame him for changing his number or wanting nothing to do with me. I pushed him away when all he'd tried to do was love me and help me and be there for me. I ran away from him like he was an escaped criminal or something. I was wrong, dead wrong.

I was so brokenhearted that my sons thought I was sick. I didn't comb my hair or walk outside my house for days. Then came another phone call from Marli. I was in no shape to talk to her, but I answered the call nonetheless.

"What's going on?" Marli asked before I could even say, "Hello."

"What are you talking about?" I asked, trying to sound nonchalant, but inside, I was literally dying from heartache.

"Well, did you call him? It's been like over a week since we last talked."

"Call who?" I said, knowing full well that she was referring to Michael.

"Oh, Lord, you didn't, did you? That's why you're playing these doggone word games."

"I... I tried to call him."

"*Tried?* There's no try. You either did or you didn't."

"You sound like Yoda from *Star Wars*."

"Carla..."

"I called him."

"And?"

I squeezed my eyes shut. "His number is no longer in service."

"What?! Well, what are you gonna do?"

"Nothing. I mean, what else can I do besides what I've been doing—sitting here feeling sick about it?"

"Carla, you have a computer and internet access. Find him!"

"He changed his number, Marli, and he didn't call me to give me the new one. As a matter of fact, he hasn't called me at all in months. I haven't talked to him since that day he showed up at my parents' house. He obviously doesn't want to be found. He doesn't want anything to do with me. Maybe..."

"Maybe, what?"

"Maybe he's better off without me, anyway."

"You don't really believe that, do you?"

I shrugged. "Sort of."

The other end fell silent. As a matter of fact, it was silent for so long, I thought Marli had hung up. "Hello?" I said.

"Do you love him?" Marli finally asked.

"I don't even know," I replied.

"Yeah, you know. You're a grown woman. You know what love feels like. Stop thinking about what makes sense. I know it doesn't seem to make sense to fall in love with someone you barely know, but love *never* makes sense. Believe me, I know. Do you love him? In your heart, do you love him?"

As tears filled my eyes, I said, "Yes, I do."

"Do you believe that he loves you?"

I nodded as I wiped a tear from my cheek. "Yes."

"He pursued you. He drove all the way to your parents' house. Now, it's your turn. Find him. Tell him how you feel."

"But—"

"If you love him, he's worth going the extra mile. If you love him, you won't stop until you find him."

I held the phone and cried.

"Do you hear me, Carla?"

"Yes."

"You gave Bryan too many chances, and you barely gave Michael one, and Lord knows he's more deserving."

I couldn't even respond. She was almost too correct with that statement.

"I know I'm right, and so do you. Now, get off this damn phone and get to work," she said. "Be aggressive like my old friend who would stop at nothing to get what she wanted. Besides, you know you need a date for Tiffany's wedding."

I laughed lightly through my tears. "I almost forgot your baby was getting married."

"Well, you need to remember. I expect to see you there, dressed to kill, with the man you love on your arm. *Find him.* Love you, girl, and I'll talk to you later."

"Okay. Love you, too."

After we ended the call and I pulled myself together, I searched the UALR website to see if Michael was listed as a faculty member. It didn't take long to find him. There he was, smiling at me from my computer screen—*Mr. Michael Ross, M.A. - History Instructor/Doctoral Candidate*. I stared at that picture for so long, my vision began to blur. Next to his name was the phone number to his office. I grabbed my phone and dialed the number only to get a voicemail announcement that nearly made my heart stop.

"Hi, you've reached the office of Michael Ross. I am currently on a leave of absence and will be out of the office indefinitely. For assistance, please contact the history department chairperson directly..."

My brain felt like it was twisting into a knot. What was going on? First he changed his number, now a leave of absence? I sat there feeling defeated for ten minutes before deciding to call Mrs. Cook.

"Hello?" sang her familiar voice.

"Mrs. Cook? This is Carla Tooley. Do you remember me?"

"Of course! You're Marli's lovely friend. How are you, sweetie?"

I smiled. "I'm fine. How are you?"

"I'm doing as well as I can."

"That's good. Um, Mrs. Cook, I was wondering if you could help me with something."

"Well, I'll certainly try. What do you need, honey?"

"Um, I was wondering if the man who stayed in the cabin next to me, Mr. Ross, had left you a forwarding address."

"Well, no, he didn't."

I sank into the cushion of my sofa and sighed. "Oh, okay."

"No, he sure didn't. But I guess there wasn't any need for him to do that since he never left."

I sat up straight, my heart thundering in my chest. "What?"

"He never left. He's still in that cabin right now today."

I held my hand to my mouth and rocked back and forth on the sofa while I silently shouted for joy.

"Honey, are you still there?"

"Yes, ma'am. Thank you. Thank you so much!"

"Well, you're welcome."

"Um, I've got to go, Mrs. Cook. I'll talk to you later."

The rest of that day went by very quickly. I snatched off the ratty clothing I'd been wearing for days, took a shower, brushed my teeth, and fixed my hair. I got dressed and spent most of the day rehearsing what I'd say to him, finally settling on, "I love you," and "I'm sorry."

I picked my boys up from school and dropped them off at my parents' house, though Derek was irritated by the fact that I still made them stay with a babysitter. I just wasn't comfortable with them being alone in that house out on the river.

Then I hit the highway and drove the nearly two-hour path to Cook Lake. When I arrived, his truck was gone. I knocked on the door, but, of course, there was no answer. I sat in my vehicle for a while, but it was December, and it was cold. It was even threatening to snow, so after an hour of waiting, I drove down to Mrs. Cook's and got the key to Marli's cabin, having decided to wait there until he returned. Another hour passed, then another. I was quickly losing faith. Maybe I should've told Mrs. Cook that I was coming and had her tell Michael. But I hadn't done that, because I was afraid he'd tell her to tell me he didn't want to see me. In my mind, surprising him was the best plan. But sitting in my friend's cabin with no food and no Michael, I began to question my judgment.

Around 10:30 P.M., I finally drifted off to sleep, hoping he'd see my vehicle when he pulled up and come looking for me. Hope was all I had left.

***

The first thing I did when I woke up the next morning was rush to the front porch and check to see if Michael was home. My face and my hopes fell when I saw that his driveway was still empty. Where was he? Where in the world could he have been? Had he ever made it home that night? If not, was he with someone? Had he moved on?

I walked back into the cabin with nothing but despair and defeat in my heart. I slumped down on the sofa, clutched my empty stomach, and cried like a baby. I wailed for the better part of an hour, mourning the loss of what was probably the best man I'd ever known. I cried and cried until I cried myself back to sleep.

An hour later, I woke up to the sound of a loud engine. I rushed to the door to see that it was only an old car passing by on the dirt road. My hopes fell again until I noticed Michael's truck in his driveway. My first instinct was to rush over to his place and beat the door down, but then I remembered I'd been crying earlier and that I probably looked a hot mess, not to mention the fact that I hadn't eaten in hours and that my breath was probably kicking *hard*.

I trotted to the bathroom, washed my face, ran my fingers through my braids, and popped a peppermint I found in my purse into my mouth in hopes of freshening my breath. Then I tried to calm my nerves. I took a few deep breaths, said a quick prayer, and made my way to his cabin. I knocked on the door and held my breath as I waited—no answer.

I turned and looked at the old truck sitting in front of the cabin just to be sure I hadn't imagined it. There it sat, rust and all, Cherokee Nation license plate adorning the front as always. I frowned as I knocked again—no answer, *again*. I moved to the side and peered through the slightly open curtain. I didn't see him. I sighed and felt tears begin to fill my eyes as I stepped off of the porch and walked around to the back of the house. My breath made clouds in the cold air as I knocked on the back door. Yet again, no answer. I leaned my weary head against the door and wept quietly. Then I lifted my head and began to search my surroundings with my eyes. There was no sign of him at all. The whole situation felt like a cruel joke. He'd been there, and I'd missed him, and he hadn't tried to come over to my cabin. Obviously, he was done with me. I needed to leave. There was no use in staying. It would be better for me to go back home and go on living just the way I had for the past six months—without him—than to keep humiliating myself.

I walked back over to Marli's cabin, locked it up, and climbed into my car. As I backed out of the driveway, on my way to Mrs. Cook's to return the key, I pulled out my cell phone to call and let my mother know I was on my way back home. As I put my car in drive, I noticed something—the trail. I noticed the trail that led into the woods, the one I'd walked with Michael. The one that led to the field of lavender. I pulled my car back into the driveway and climbed out of it.

I was afraid of snakes and spiders. I was afraid of walking through a forest alone. I half-expected the boogie man to jump out from behind one of those tall trees at any moment. But the one thing that scared me most was the thought of losing Michael Ross forever. That was the stuff that nightmares were really made of.

I walked slowly, trying to remember the path we'd taken to the lavender field that day. A few times, I thought I was lost, but after about twenty minutes of uncertain travel, I made it. The flowers were gone, replaced by the sad emptiness of winter. I sighed as the earlier scene replayed itself—no Michael, not even a sign of him having been there. At that point, I was so exhausted from sheer disappointment and lack of nutrition, I slumped to the ground and sat there and cried. In all my life I hadn't cried as much as I had in those couple of hours. I shoved my hands into the pockets of my short jacket and just sat there. The cold didn't bother me, because by that time, I was numb from heartache and frustration.

My mother's words echoed in my mind: *"You can make him wait if you want to, but you better hope you don't make him wait too long and end up losing him."*

When my tears finally dried, I sat there and listened to the quietness surrounding me. It would've been peaceful had my heart not been breaking more and more with each beat. I sat there for a long while with my eyes shut, trying to calm my tattered nerves, and then it began to snow. *Great*, I thought, *now I have to drive back home in this mess.* That's when I heard sounds that made my breath halt—the crunching of leaves, the snapping of a twig. I opened my eyes and slowly turned my head toward the forest. There he stood. His hair hung nearly to his waist. Had he let it grow for me? His broad chest was covered by a plaid, flannel shirt; faded, ripped jeans covered his long legs, a look of concern covered his face. He was such a beautiful sight, a sight for sore eyes.

I slowly got to my feet and faced him. "You're so beautiful," I said softly.

He stared at me, shifted his eyes to the ground then back to me, and said, "Thank you. So are you."

Then we just stood there for a few minutes, staring at each other. I could almost hear his thoughts, because something inside of me told me that they echoed mine—*Is this real or am I dreaming?*

"I've been trying to reach you. You changed your number, and I couldn't reach you at the university. I've been going out of my mind trying to find you," I finally said.

"Why? Why have you been trying to find me?"

"Because... I missed you."

He dropped his eyes, didn't return the sentiment, but I understood why.

"What happened? Why'd you change your number, leave your job?" I asked.

"I needed time to myself," he said.

"Time for what?"

"Time to forget you."

My heart lurched. "Did you? Did you forget me?"

He shook his head slightly. "What do you think?"

"Michael, I'm... I'm sorry. I'm *so sorry* for pushing you away. It was a mistake. It was a *huge* mistake to treat you like that. All you did was love me. You saved me over and over again."

He didn't say a word.

I moved close enough to him to feel his body heat in the open winter air. "I was literally out of my mind when I rejected you. I'm truly sorry, Michael. I hope you'll forgive me."

His eyes met mine. "I forgave you a long time ago. Forgiving is easy. It's the forgetting that's hard."

I reached up and placed my hand gently on his cheek. "I know it is, but it's a little easier when you love someone, when the love is real, right?"

He clenched his jaw and averted his gaze, but didn't reply.

"I love you, Michael."

He glanced at me. "Are you sure? Do you even know what that means?"

I nodded. "Yes, I'm sure, and yes, I know what it means. Do you still love me?"

He sighed and turned his back to me.

I reached for him, then withdrew my hand. "Do you?" I repeated.

Please say yes... please say yes, I pleaded silently. *God, you gon' have to help me if he says no.*

He faced me again. "More than ever."

I moved closer to him, wrapped my arms around him, and rested my head on his chest. "Thank God, because I also wanted to tell you that I figured out what my dream is."

He wrapped his long arms around me and pulled me close to him. "What's your dream?"

I looked up at him and smiled. "Where's the ring?"

"What ring?"

"The *ring*, Michael. The one I saw the night Bryan showed up at my cabin."

"Oh, *that* ring. Why do you want to know?"

"Because... I want you to put it on me. My dream is for you to put that ring on my finger and be with me forever."

"What makes you think I still have it?"

"I... I hope you do. *Do* you still have it?

He grinned as he dug into the hip pocket of his jeans and unearthed the ring.

My eyes widened. It was absolutely beautiful. "You actually have it with you?" I asked.

He shrugged. "When I saw your car back at the cabin, I knew you were here for me. I figured I'd bring it with me."

"Then, where were you? I knocked on your door."

"I was out here, waiting for you. I watched you come here."

"Why didn't you say anything?"

"I just wanted to look at you for a while. You know, spy on you like you used to spy on me?"

I rolled my eyes. "Why do you have to bring up the past?"

He grinned and shrugged his shoulders again. "For the same reason you always feel the need to ask so many questions, I guess."

"Well, are you going to get down on one knee and ask me properly?"

He reached for my hand and slid the ring on my finger. "No, because you already asked *me* by showing up here, and I'm saying yes." He held my face in his hands and gazed into my eyes. "I love you, Awenasa."

I smiled up at him. "You said you'd tell me what that really means."

"It means, 'my home.' You're my home, Carla. I think you always have been."

"You're my home, too. And I love you more than you'll ever know, Michael Ross."

He leaned in and kissed me for a long, lingering moment. Soft snow swirled around us as the wind began to pick up. "Hmm, well, that's good to hear. So all you want from me is forever, huh?"

I nodded. "That's it. Oh, and I want you to promise me something."

He slid his hands up and down my back. "What's that?"

"I want you to promise that you'll skinny dip for me every

night—in a lake, a pool, the tub, *anywhere*."

He grinned widely. "I'll do that for you if you promise to do the same thing for me."

I wrapped my arms around him, squeezed tightly, and said, "Deal."

Discussion Questions

1. How did you feel about Carla and Bryan attempting to reconcile in the beginning of the book? Would you have given him another chance? Why or why not?

2. Were you shocked by Bryan's violent behavior?

3. Do you think Carla should have reported the rape? Why or why not?

4. What was your reaction to the motel scene? What would you have done in the same situation?

5. What was your first impression of Michael Ross?

6. Did you understand why Carla protected Bryan, or were you frustrated with her?

7. Do you think it was right for Carla to tell Shauna Parker about her husband? Why or why not?

8. Why do you think Carla had a mental breakdown?

9. What did you like most about the book? What did you like least about the book?

10. Who was your favorite character? Your least favorite character?

11. Overall, did you enjoy the book? Did it change any of your views? Did you learn something new?

12. Would you recommend this book to others?

For Rape Crisis/Intervention Information, visit:

https://www.rainn.org/

For information regarding the Cherokee Nation, visit:

http://www.cherokee.org/

To learn more about Author Adrienne Thompson, visit,
http://adriennethompsonwrites.webs.com

Sign up for Adrienne's newsletter here: http://eepurl.com/jnDmH

Follow Adrienne on Twitter!

https://twitter.com/A_H_Thompson

Like Adrienne on Facebook!

https://www.facebook.com/AdrienneThompsonWrites

Follow Adrienne on Pinterest!

http://www.pinterest.com/ahthompsn/

Also by Adrienne Thompson

The *Bluesday* Series:

Bluesday

Lovely Blues

Blues In The Key Of B

Locked out of Heaven (Tomeka's Story – A Bluesday Continuation)

The *Been So Long* Series:

Rapture (A Been So Long Prequel)

If (Wasif's Story) A Been So Long Prequel

Been So Long

Little Sister (Cleo's Story—a companion novel to Been So Long)

Been So Long 2 (Body and Soul)

Been So Long III (Whatever It Takes)

Stand-alone novels:

See Me

Your Love Is King

When You've Been Blessed (Feels Like Heaven)

Anthology:

Just Between Us (Inspiring Stories by Women)

All books are available at amazon.com, barnesandnoble.com, and kobobooks.com

Excerpt from *Home:*

Coming in 2015

I sat and tried not to let my eyes glaze over as another young, attractive, African American female rattled off her qualifications to me in an effort to convince me to hire her as my administrative assistant, since unfortunately, I'd had to fire Alma. One night was all I was trying to give her. But after that night, she started strutting around the office like she owned the place. Typed on the keypad of her cell phone more than she ever did the computer. I just couldn't afford to keep her, or her attitude, around after I told her we were through.

So there I sat, just three months after hiring her, seeking her replacement, listening to Jazzmine, who was thicker than a six-pack of Snickers. As she rambled on about her experience in Atlanta, I penciled an "x" beside her name. She wouldn't do at all. She was too fine. So were Tammy, LaShay, and Amber—fine, finer, and finest. I had to find someone unattractive to hire if I was going to keep any help around here.

I stood and shook her hand once the interview was over, gave her the "I'll be in touch" lie, and settled back down in my executive chair. I straightened my tie and released a long, belabored sigh. More interviews tomorrow. I was just about to pray that a homely girl would show up at my door with impeccable organizational and typing skills when my cell phone rang. I recognized the area code but not the number. The call was coming from Arkansas.

My entire body stiffened. The only time I got calls from Arkansas was when my mother, who was suffering from advanced Alzheimer's disease, happened to get ahold of the phone and hit the speed-dial for my number, and even then, she swore I was my daddy, and those conversations were awkward to say the least. If she wasn't whispering sweet nothings to me, she was crying or cussing about some woman she was sure I/my father was with. The only other time I got a call was on my birthday, and that call came from my Aunt Golinda. Well, it wasn't my birthday, so it was probably my mother. Maybe she'd gotten her hands on someone else's phone. But as much as I loved that woman, and I truly did, it was almost too painful for me to speak to her, knowing she had no idea who I was.

"Hello?" I answered softly.

"Yes, is this Mr. Ivan Spencer?"

I sat up straight in my seat. That was not my mother's voice nor my aunt's. It was the voice of a young woman, and my interest was involuntarily piqued. "Yes, it is. Who's this?" I asked, putting on my official voice.

"Mr. Spencer, this is Kenesha, your mama's daytime aide. Look, it's time for me to go home, and the girl who s'posed to come in after me done called in. The company don't have no substitute aide to send for the evening. They been tryna call your daddy, Mr. Wardell, but they can't get him, and he ain't here. I would stay, but I gotta get home."

I felt my head tighten. What the hell was I paying these folks for if they couldn't find a replacement? My mother couldn't be left alone. Up until three years ago, my sister, Imogene, had been staying with Mama and Daddy and taking care of Mama around the clock.

Then she decided to go to the casino in Mississippi with some of her church friends and hooked up with a jack-leg preacher. The next thing I knew, she'd run off with him to Mississippi. She got married and hadn't been home since. I couldn't be mad at her, though. While I left home at eighteen, Imogene had never been further than twenty miles out of town up until the time she was thirty-five, when she ran off with her preacher man.

"Um," I said, trying to sound calm, since it wasn't this young lady's fault that her boss was incompetent. "Let me see if I can get in touch with someone to come and relieve you. Can I call you back at this number?"

"Sure. Your mama done hid the house phone. That's why I had to call on my own phone."

"I see. Well, give me a few minutes, and I promise I'll call you back."

"Yessir."

I hung up and dialed my aunt's number. She answered with her usual, "Praise God."

"Hey, auntie. It's your favorite nephew. How you doing?" I said, trying to sound as sweet as I could.

"Ivan! Boy, is that you? I ain't heard from you in so long! How you doin', baby? Done got married yet?"

I chuckled. "No, ma'am. Look, I was needing to ask you a favor."

"You know there ain't nothin' I won't do for you, baby. What is it?"

"Auntie, can you go sit with Mama this evening? The girl from the agency called in sick."

After a long pause, she said, "Where your daddy at?"

"I don't know, auntie. The girl that called just said he wasn't there."

"Probably got his sorry behind out somewhere cheating on my poor, senile sister. Son-of-a—"

"Uh, auntie, can you do it for me? Sit with her? I'd really appreciate it."

"Of course I will. But you know what? You need to come see your mama. She ain't doing well, Ivan. She gettin' worse by the day. The other day I went by there, and she thought I was Imogene."

"Yes, ma'am. I'm planning on doing that."

"Don't plan, baby. *Do it.* I got a feeling time ain't long for her. You need to come spend some time with her 'fo she go."

I closed my eyes and nodded. "Yes, ma'am. I am. Thank you so much for doing this."

"No 'thank you' necessary. She my sister. My only living sibling."

"Yes, ma'am."

I ended the call and dialed the nurse aide's number.

"Hello?" she answered.

"Yes, this is Ivan Spencer. My aunt is on her way to relieve you. She should be there shortly. Can you stay with my mom until she gets there? I'm more than willing to compensate you for the extra time."

"Yessir, I can stay."

"Okay, thank you."

"You're welcome."

I hung up and grabbed my jacket. I left my office early that day and tried to dismiss any thoughts of my mother and her demented mind from my own.

Excerpt from *Ain't Nobody*

Coming early 2015

I was sitting in my mother's living room, enjoying our weekly visit, when she decided to ruin it for me.

"He calls me every day. Sound like he's crying half the time," she said out of the blue.

"Who?" I asked as I picked up a *People* magazine from the coffee table and studied the cover like I was going to be quizzed on it later.

"You know who. *Quincy*. When you gon' make up with him?"

"I'm not. We're over."

Mama leaned forward in her recliner and shook her finger at me. "A man is hard to come by—especially one with a job. He ain't got no kids, and he's got his own place. I don't know what else you could want, Alex."

I turned my head toward the TV, which was playing a Tyler Perry DVD with the volume muted. "Commitment."

"Ain't y'all engaged?"

"Yes, but if I leave it up to Quincy, we'll be engaged *forever*. I mean, by the time you were my age, you'd already been married twice. Farrah's younger than me, and she's already been married *and* divorced. And look at Gwin. She's been married practically since the beginning of time. I just want my chance to have a family."

Mama frowned. "Well, hell, ain't none of that worth bragging about. Farrah's divorced, I've been married twice, and Gwin's husband won't even go to church with her. What kind of marriage is that? I don't know what you think marriage is, but let me be the first to tell you, it ain't no fairy tale. It's a bunch of work. Sometimes it's worth the trouble, and sometimes it's not. But one thing's for sure, you ain't gon' get no closer to marrying the man by quitting him. That just don't make no sense to me."

I sighed. "Mama, I really don't want to discuss this." I pointed to the TV. "Which one is this? *I Can Do Bad All by Myself?*"

"Naw, *Diary of a Mad Black Woman*. Alex, you're making a mistake."

Before I could answer, I heard the front door open and close, and seconds later, my younger sister, Farrah, walked in wearing tight jeans and a tank top. She was six years my junior, and she was gorgeous. She was petite with the smoothest brown skin, and I'd literally kill for her body. She'd already had one husband, two kids, and two baby daddies, but she looked like she was still in high school.

"Hey, y'all," she said as she plopped down on the sofa next to me. "Where the kids?"

"They in the family room playing one of those video games," Mama said.

"Well, can they stay here tonight? I got some stuff I need to do," Farrah asked.

"*Someone* you need to do," I said under my breath.

"I heard that, Alex. Don't hate on me just because you ain't got no man. Oh, that's right, you *had* one, but you threw him away," Farrah countered.

"You have no idea what you're talking about. Why don't you worry about raising your kids, and stop leaving them on Mama all the time," I said through my teeth.

"That's enough!" Mama shouted.

We were all startled by the ringing of the doorbell.

"I'll get it," I said. I cut my eyes at Farrah as I headed to the front door. Mama shook her head as I passed by her. I opened the door and wanted to scream. Mama had planned this, and I knew it. Standing on the other side of the door was Quincy.

"Mama! I think you have company!" I yelled as Quincy stood there and stared at me.

"No, I don't. That's *your* company," she called back.

Made in the USA
San Bernardino, CA
04 September 2018